Death Money

Also by Henry Chang

Chinatown Beat
Year of the Dog
Red Jade

Death Money

Henry Chang

Copyright © 2014 by Henry Chang

Published by
Soho Press, Inc.
853 Broadway
New York, NY 10003

Library of Congress Cataloging-in-Publication Data

Chang, Henry, 1951–
Death money / Henry Chang.

ISBN 978-1-61695-532-8
eISBN 978-1-61695-352-2

1. Yu, Jack (Fictitious character)—Fiction. 2. New York (N.Y.). Police
Department—Fiction. 3. Chinese—United States—Fiction. 4. Chinatown
(New York, N.Y.)—Fiction. I. Title.
PS3603.H35728D43 2014
813'.6—dc23   2013045378

Printed in the United States of America

10 9 8 7 6 5 4 3 2 1

Flow

IT WAS 7 A.M. when Detective Jack Yu stepped into the frigid dawn spreading over Sunset Park. A slate-gray Brooklyn morning with single-digit temperatures driven by wind shrieking off the East River. He scanned Eighth Avenue for the Chinese *see gay* radio cars but saw none, only a couple of Taipan minibuses, *sai ba*, queued up a block away from the Double Eight Cantonese restaurant.

The wind gusted fierce and he regretted not wearing one of his Army Airborne sapper hats. The minibuses were slower than the car service jocks, but with early morning rush-hour traffic already streaming into Manhattan, it wouldn't make much difference. And although he'd wanted the quiet solitude of one of the black radio cars to review his thoughts for his appointment with the NYPD-assigned shrink at the Ninth Precinct, he'd also felt the need to be *connected*, wanted some proximity to Chinese people, his own people, *civilians*. The twenty-five-minute bouncy rush across the BQE to Manhattan's Chinatown, an undulating ride to people's jobs, schools, to whatever their piece of the Gum Shan, Gold Mountain, demanded of them, would work as well, he decided.

"*Leung kwai*," the driver said in Mandarin, and Jack handed him the two dollars.

Jack took a window seat and shifted his Colt Detective Special along the small of his back so that it wouldn't poke him when he sat against the worn seat cushions. A Hong Kong variety show played over a monitor behind the driver, more static than music, beneath the banter and cell-phone conversations of the other dozen passengers. *Chinese-American life on the expressway*, Jack mused. With Pa's passing, he was alone at the end of the Yu family line.

He could see the Verrazano Bridge fading in the distance, *the guinea gangplank*, as they swerved away from the Brooklyn Chinatown.

The minibus shifted gears for the highway. From his window he saw broad residential tracts, industrial parks, high rises leading the way to the office buildings of downtown Brooklyn.

Housing projects and ghetto neighborhoods rushing by.

Jack took a deep *shaolin* boxer's breath through his nose and tried to collect his thoughts. It had been six months since his return to the Chinatown precinct, before his old man passed away. His Fifth Precinct cases had taken him to West Coast Chinatowns and back to New York City, but along the way he'd processed a dozen dead bodies, had been beaten by Triad thugs, mauled by a pit bull, and shot twice. He'd also killed two men. All this, especially the last two, would be of interest to the shrink. He was advised that *it'd be good to talk about it*.

Cemeteries, graffitied rooftops, whistling by. The minibus shifting gears again. Billboards beckoning poor people to Atlantic City to gamble away their monthly checks.

And then, just as suddenly, the memory that there was a woman in his life now, a fiery Chinatown lawyer going through a messy divorce. They had become drinking buddies, then graduated to *friends*, and finally, they'd crossed the line. They'd shared a weekend together, and now he couldn't keep Alexandra, *Alex*, out of his mind.

The minibus made its gassy sprint through the edge of Brooklyn toward the Manhattan Bridge, and before he knew it he saw the icy East River below.

He thought he'd have known better than to get involved with someone going through an acrimonious divorce, with a young daughter, sure to face custody and support issues. But in light of all that had happened in Chinatown, and after, when they'd been by each other's side, there was no longer any need to tiptoe around their feelings. They'd crossed the line that separates friends from lovers, and in the back of his cop's mind, he wondered what the consequences would be.

The river wind reminded him of the salty scent of silk sheets, curled damp around Alex as she lay naked next to him.

He wanted to bring her something sweet.

Jack hoped to squeeze in an early bird meeting with Captain Marino, CO of the Fifth Precinct, before picking up some desserts from the Tofu King around the corner from the station house. He'd still have time to drop off the sweets at Alex's Lower East Side storefront office, then catch a bus north for the shrink session at the Ninth Precinct. Half the plan was ambitious, *touch and go*. He decided to follow the possibilities and forgo whatever didn't go with the morning's plans.

The minibus churned across the metalwork of the span and descended into Chinatown. It careened onto Division Street and dropped its passengers off beneath the desolate bridge.

Division was a wind tunnel channeling icy gusts off the high-rise curves of Confucius Towers, whipping onto the streets below. Alex's apartment at Confucius Towers was where they'd given in to intimacy.

Jack zipped his Gore-Tex parka up to his chin, lowered his head into the wind, and went toward Bowery. The Fifth Precinct was four blocks away, close to the Tofu King. Alex liked the *bok tong go* and the *dao foo fa* treats, he knew. He marched on until he turned the corner of the Towers. His cheeks felt windburned, his lips frostbitten, but Bayard Street was just another block. He wondered if Captain Marino had arrived early.

He exhaled steam through his upturned collar. The precinct was just a dash across Bowery now, the businesses on the empty boulevard still shuttered in the frozen Chinatown dawn. The Tofu King, however, would be open for the early bird special, a two-for-one deal on bricks of fresh tofu to kick off the day. *Baker's hours.* The Chinatown grandmothers bought *jong* and tofu early, before the free bowl of congee breakfast at the Seniors' Center.

At the corner of Elizabeth Alley, Jack didn't see the captain's car outside the station house, but maybe one of the squad had already moved it to parking.

"THE CAPTAIN IN yet?" Jack asked.

The uniformed officer stepping out of the station house hesitated and regarded Jack with suspicion before answering, "Haven't seen him, but we got CompStat this morning."

Fuhgeddaboudit, Jack imagined Marino saying. Computer statistics analysis, *CompStat*, could take the entire morning, if not the whole day, with Commanding Officer Marino answering to the issues and anomalies of the Chinatown precinct.

So forget the early bird catch-up meet with the good captain.

Jack turned and went down Bayard toward the Tofu King.

From the corner of Mott he could already see the steamy air gushing out of the tofu factory, the morning belch from hot bean products cooking out of the vats and slats behind the front counter and refrigerator cases.

He'd want to pay for the sweet desserts before Billy Bow, who'd inherited the third-generation family business, could dramatically refuse his money. Billy, his last neighborhood friend, *eyes and ears in Chinatown,* an embittered divorcé. It was just a few bucks that Jack was happy to pay, but Billy refused to value their friendship against the products of his lifeblood, tofu. So they regularly bought each other drinks at Grampa's bar, fortifying their Chinatown bond. Two budding alcoholics feeding off each other.

Billy had an interesting take on Chinese marriage and never needed much prodding to complain about his ex-wife.

JACK STEPPED INTO the foggy shop front and grabbed two plastic containers of *bok tong go* and *wong tong go,* angling toward the hot *dao foo fa* and determined to pay before Billy Bow noticed.

The cashier was on the phone, but after she hung up she refused his money in her guttural Toishanese and signaled to the next customers in line.

"Saw you on the surveillance camera," said Billy, stepping out from behind the steaming vats of beans. "You're an early bird today?" He eyed Jack's bag of desserts. "That for the lawyer chick again?" He grinned. "I warned you. *Baggage*."

He meant Alex's grade-school daughter, Chloe, aka Kimberly.

Homeboy Billy, Jack mused, *his eyes and ears on the street but his nose always in other people's business.*

"Tell me again," Jack countered, "why you got divorced."

"Whaddya watching Oprah again? There's a *hundred* reasons. How many you want?"

"I got time for one," Jack said, grinning.

Six Skirts, Ten Shirts

BILLY CHECKED THE steam vats as he began. "Okay, for one thing, we had laundry problems." Jack narrowed his eyes skeptically.

"No, really." Billy continued, "You know my little girls went to Transfiguration, right? Catholic school." Jack knew, as most Chinatown residents did, the Church of the Transfiguration on Mott Street had served the Chinatown area for more than a hundred years and was a popular alternative to the rough public-school education Jack had gotten.

Billy continued, "So the girls got these school uniforms. Shirts, skirts, sweaters, like that. Two sets each, rotate from week to week, right?" Jack nodded, urging him on. "Well, *wifey*, she's having everything *dry-cleaned*, dig? And after a while I see that it's costing me more than the fuckin' parking space at Confucius! And don't get me started, that's another fuckin' matter. Anyway, so I took over the laundry duties. Got everything washed at Danny Chong's Laundromat.

Everything comes back folded, neat. Then I do whatever ironing myself, right? Cool."

Jack took a *shaolin patience* breath as he nodded again, still refusing to interrupt Billy.

"So one day I'm ironing, right? Just the touch-up stuff. And she comes over to *supervise*, starts telling me I'm doing it *wrong*. 'Collar first,' she says. 'Then the cuffs, and sleeves,' blah, blah, right? *This* advice from the mother who never lifted an iron for her girls. *Supervising* me. 'And you have to put a towel under the buttons,' she says. 'Yeah?' I said, 'Who says?' '*Martha Stewart*,' she says. She saw it on cable. '*Fuck* Martha Stewart,' I said. 'This is how *I* been doing it, not *you*. Between the *yum cha* with the ladies, and the *da mah jerk*, I don't see you ironing *shit*.'"

"What did she say to that?" Jack ventured.

"Called me an ignorant Chinatown lowlife."

"No shit." Jack laughed.

"Not for nothing, Jacky," Billy began, his jaw clenched, "our people got history doing laundry in America. So telling a Chinaman how to iron a shirt is like telling a nigger how to eat a watermelon."

Jack shook his head and snickered in spite of himself.

A timer went off somewhere, and Billy turned to check the hot slats of tofu. Jack glanced at the wall clock and saw his chance to exit. Still, he felt bad for Billy, the bitter divorcé who found solace in loose women and the occasional whore at Chao's.

"Gotta roll," Jack said.

"Breeze, homeboy." Billy grinned, looking up from the hot mist. "And remember. *She's baggage*."

AJA

THE FREEZING WIND seemed even more brutal as Jack stepped out of the steamy tofu shop, and he went east on Canal at a brisk pace, passing the firehouse and the Buddhist temple, going through the old junkie parks that led into *Loisaida*, the Lower East Side. He clenched his jaw against the cold, and soon the renovated bodega that had become Alex's office came into view.

The sign over the storefront read ASIAN AMERICAN JUSTICE ADVOCACY and a banner with the letters AJA fluttered in the wind. Jack could see Alex through the front window, in her back office. She wasn't alone.

Jack went in quietly and placed the bag of desserts on the receptionist's desk. He recognized the man standing in Alex's office as Assistant District Attorney Bang Sing, a prosecutor he'd worked with on a previous Chinatown case. Sing looked pissed off, and Jack overheard him say, "Look, I only got assigned this case because I'm Chinese. And you know it. They want to put a yellow face on it," he groused. "What are you gonna do? So if there *is* a tape, I need to see it. And if I have to, I'll drop the damn case. It's a no-win situation for me."

Alex noticed Jack's quiet arrival with a nod, but kept her game face on.

Jack knew what ADA Sing was referring to. The city had resurrected an obscure ban on fireworks for future traditional Chinatown celebrations, like the Chinese New Year. Many residents and activists were outraged, but one Chinese-American Iraq War veteran had protested the ban by lighting up a strand of tiny ladyfinger firecrackers on the steps of City Hall. He got arrested and was charged with trespassing, disorderly conduct, inciting to riot, and resisting arrest. Then the sudden appearance of a home videotape of the incident put the lie to the NYPD charges of inciting riot and resisting arrest. The tape cast doubt on disorderly conduct and trespassing as well, and now ADA Bang Sing was going to have to eat one for the blue team. Jack knew it would be a hard pill to swallow for the driven Chinese ADA, and he sure wouldn't be happy with Alex for taking the Chinese veteran's side *pro bono*, along with the local American Legion Post. The incident had aroused a sense of pride in Jack, but as a cop he felt tainted by police misconduct.

ADA Sing left Alex's office in a huff and barely nodded to Jack as he passed, buttoning up his black trench coat on the way out.

Jack took the desserts off the receptionist's desk and went into Alex's office. He could tell she was stressed even as she welcomed him with a small smile, knowing what was in the Tofu King bag.

"What's up, lady?" Jack said as he placed the treats on her desk.

"Same old crap," Alex answered sweetly. "You know, *police* misconduct, false allegations, trumped-up charges. The usual NYPD game."

Jack took a breath and teased, "There's always three sides to every story."

"Don't even try *Rashomon* on me," Alex warned. "We have a videotape of what *really* happened at City Hall, made by a friend of the 'perpetrator.' And it's going to exonerate my client, who, by the way, is a war veteran. A hero, mind you."

Jack shook his head, though he agreed with her.

"This one's going to be a slam dunk," Alex said matter-of-factly.

Jack took her hand in his, felt the warm softness there. "Cold," she said. "You came a long way. How's *your* morning going?"

"Better, now that I'm here." She rubbed his hand in hers, but they separated awkwardly as the receptionist entered the storefront.

"Thanks for the sweet stuff," Alex said quietly.

"Sure," Jack answered as the receptionist booted up her desktop computer. "Call you later." He exited her office and left the storefront without conversing with the receptionist. *Catch an M15 north*, he was thinking, heading for the Ninth Precinct.

Floating

THEY CAME TO the railing that separates parkland from the seawall embankment, looking out over the Harlem River.

"Jeez, it's fuckin' freezing," cursed Patrolman Mulligan.

It was an hour before the end of the shift in Manhattan North, and it wasn't the first time that the Thirty-Second Precinct, the *Three-Two*, had to fish a floater out of the Harlem River.

"Let's get in the rowboat," the taller man, Sergeant Cohen, said. "It's only about fifty yards out."

At its narrowest point, the Harlem River was still almost a quarter-mile wide, about four city blocks across, and as the two cops squinted against the river wind, they could see a bulky shape entangled in tree branches near the middle of the river. The limbs were snagged up against some chunky ice floes.

"Time for a close-up," the sergeant said.

Sergeant Cohen was in his forties, and his gray, ball-bearing pupils focused on the aluminum Columbia University rowboat at the water's edge. The land part was operated by the Parks Department.

"Let's go, kid," the sergeant said to the patrolman. "The river's half frozen anyway."

PO Mulligan, twenty years younger, held the rowboat steady as Sergeant Cohen stepped in and squatted. Mulligan shoved off, jumping in as the rowboat skimmed in the direction of the submerged tree stump.

Mulligan pulled up his blue NYPD-monogrammed turtleneck. "Freezing," he repeated, breathing evenly as he set the oars.

They could hear the distant crackle of radio broadcasts as he started rowing through the surface ice. The patrolman pulled on the oars, figuring the distance at a couple dozen strokes.

The radio sounds got louder, until out of the gray wash came the Harbor Unit, a twin-engine Detroit fast-boat, approaching from the Bronx side of the Third Avenue Bridge. Sergeant Cohen could make out two additional uniformed officers on board and figured it quickly: *simultaneous calls and dispatch*. Multiple calls must have come through 911 emergency, from both the South Bronx and Manhattan North precincts. *Reports of a body snagged on a tree in the river.*

The Harbor Unit had been docked on the South Bronx waterfront near Hunts Point and had taken aboard the cops from the Forty-Fourth Precinct when the dispatch went out. From the fast-boat they could see the two cops in the rowboat, out from the Manhattan side, rowing closer to the bulky shape now, which was looking more like a body as they approached. The NYPD boat cut its engines, maneuvering now as its arrival sent ripples though the chunks of ice.

Sergeant Cohen could see clearly as they came within ten feet: it *was* a body, with black hair, head and torso just under the surface of the water, its right arm raised, caught in the branches of the tree. *Like he was a student, raising his arm in a classroom.* The drag of the stump, and the ice floes that had drifted around it, had kept everything in place.

The Harbor Unit boat came about and bumped up against the ice, nudging the scene more toward the Manhattan side.

Overtime, thought Sergeant Cohen. Finally he was close enough to lift the head out of the water with his baton. *Male, Asian*, he thought. *Twenty-something, maybe thirty years old.* PO Mulligan worked the oars against the ice. *A jumper? Or something else?* There was no blood that he could see. "How'd he wind up in the river?" Cohen wondered aloud.

"Hey!" one of the blues on the Harbor boat deck yelled. "Whaddya think? Someone from *your* side? You had jumpers before . . ." He looked vaguely Hispanic and also wore the stripes of a sergeant.

Sergeant Cohen barked back, "Who knows? Could have been *your* side, too. Like the Bruckner, or Hunts Point. Plenty of vics from over there."

The Harbor Unit skipper, a Nordic face, took a call over the boat radio.

There was a pause between the different cops, when all they could hear was the lapping of the currents against the ice and the whistle of the wind across the mouth of the bay. The Macombs Dam Bridge towered in the distance.

The second cop on the harbor boat, a white patrolman from the Four-Four Bronx Precinct, said, "Looks like a dead Chink to me." His Latino sergeant agreed: "*El chino.*"

PO Mulligan countered, "Could be a Jap. Or Korean." His Manhattan sense of diversity.

"They're all the same," the boat-deck patrolman said, shrugging.

"Asian," Sergeant Cohen settled on.

"*Whatever*," the Latino sarge said. "You want the case or not? All our dicks are working the club fire, anyway."

All the cops had heard about it, an enraged partygoer had returned to the Happy World Social Club with a gun and a can of gasoline, and now thirteen Central American immigrants lay dead in the smoldering ruins.

"And besides," the sarge continued from the deck, "the scene's closer to *your* side of the river now."

"Yeah, Manhattan." The Bronx patrolman grinned. "There's more Chinks in Manhattan anyways."

"Come back, Harbor Two," the boat radio crackled again.

"Negative, we don't need scuba, copy?" the blond skipper answered. More static from the radio. "We've got an Asian in the water," the skipper continued.

"Agent?" came from the radio. "What agent?"

"No, an *Asian*," repeated the skipper.

"What agency? What agent, Harbor Two?"

"Negative." The skipper paused on the open line, annoyed, when the Bronx patrolman yelled into the radio, "We got a dead Chink in the drink! Copy?"

"Oh," responded dispatch drily. "Okay. Copy that. Ten-four."

The patrolman smirked as his sergeant said toward Sergeant Cohen, "It's all yours, Manhattan."

"Wait for EMS, okay?" said dispatch.

"Copy that," answered Sergeant Cohen. "Call the house," he said to Mulligan. "Tell them we could use a Chinese, uh, *Asian* detective."

North

THE BEATEN-DOWN LANDSCAPE of the Lower East Side flashed past the bus window as Jack's cell phone sounded. It was a number he didn't recognize, but he flipped open the phone and took the call.

"Detective Yu?" asked a female dispatcher.

"Correct," Jack answered, keeping his voice even in the noise of the city bus.

"Report to Manhattan North," she said under some static.

"Come back?" Jack quietly questioned.

"Report to One Hundred Twenty-Eighth Street and Lexington. East Hamilton Park."

"Copy," Jack answered, waiting. *1-2-8 and Lex*.

"See Sergeant Cohen," came the punch line, "Hamilton Heights precinct, copy?"

"Copy that," Jack answered, anticipating the Union Square crossover in the distance. It had to be about a questionable death, he knew. But why assign a Manhattan South detective to something at the other end of Manhattan?

He watched the Ninth Precinct fade as the bus rolled north. At Union Square he dropped to the subway and caught a 4 train northbound; four stops on a twenty-minute bullet to Harlem and 125th Street.

The complexions of the passengers changed as the subway zoomed north of midtown, most people going in the opposite direction, more blacks and Latinos, minorities, bound for the Bronx.

Harlem? he wondered as the train thundered through the underground.

River

A TALL WHITE cop, a sergeant, was waiting for him at the gate to East Hamilton Park. Jack saw the insignia, with COHEN on his nameplate, and flapped open his jacket to show his gold badge.

"Detective Yu," Sergeant Cohen acknowledged.

"What do you have, Sarge?" Jack asked evenly, preferring not to question the chain of custody or command involved until later, when they got to the Thirty-Second Precinct.

"In the river," the sergeant said as he led the way to the shoreline.

Jack could see the Harbor Unit idling near the middle of the river. The wind kicked up as they went toward a metal rowboat bearing the Columbia University logo.

"After you," Sergeant Cohen said.

Jack stepped into the rowboat, dropping smoothly into a wide stance to help level the boat before sliding forward and sitting down. Sergeant Cohen pushed off and hopped aboard as they drifted forward through the choppy water. *The irony of it*, Jack thought, *a Jew rowing a Chinaman out to the middle of the Harlem River to take possession of the dead on its journey to the next life. That's how Billy Bow would see it anyway.*

Jing deng, Jack remembered, *destiny.*

The Harbor boat had blocked off the view from the Manhattan shore, shielding and securing the scene.

Jack checked his watch, made a mental note of the time: 8:49 A.M. There was a trace of salt in the wind, from far out where the river met the bay and then the Atlantic. He imagined the taste of salty seawater flowing off the sides of the Harbor boat as the sergeant rowed them forward. He noticed traffic sounds in the distance, from the shores of both north Manhattan and the South Bronx, highway traffic en route to another brutal winter day. He'd get the names and commands of the other cops later.

The river freeze seeped into Jack's jacket as they angled for the stern of the waiting boat.

"We got a male body," Sergeant Cohen offered, working the oars. "Maybe *Asian*." The word brought a cold pang of realization to Jack, knowing for certain now why he'd gotten the call.

"Snagged on a sunken tree," the sergeant continued. "After the Harbor Unit arrived, the branches shifted in the water and the body got lifted a little."

Jack nodded but was silent, taking a few *shaolin* breaths through his nose as they maneuvered around the bigger boat's stern. He patted for the plastic disposable camera he had in his jacket pocket. There was nothing else floating, nothing remarkable in the water surrounding the scene.

As they came around, Jack saw that the dragging and twisting of the submerged tree trunk had raised the body almost even with the surface of the water, caught on dead branches against large, jagged chunks of river ice.

Closer now, and Jack saw that the body wore a black bubble jacket with a black hoodie underneath. Blue jeans. The puffy bubble jacket was saturated and resembled a life jacket. The distant traffic sounds faded to the more immediate setting where Jack could now hear his own heartbeat as he lifted the head and shoulders out of the water. Male. Asian. He was already blue in the face but looked freshly dead. Jack felt for a pulse, but the man was clearly cold—frozen stiff. As hard as the body was, Jack couldn't make a guess on rigor mortis, but there were no obvious signs of trauma to the head or face and no blood, disjointed limbs, or other injuries as far as Jack could see. *A jumper?* The guy looked young but was probably in his midtwenties, Jack guessed. *He fit the profile. Looked like a student, maybe. But up here in the Harlem River? Deliveryman* was Jack's next thought. Black hair cut short at the sides, longer on top. Chinatown style, but he didn't look like a first-generation immigrant.

Jack took pictures and headshots with his free hand. Finally, he took wide shots of the scene before giving the Harbor Unit the nod to haul in the corpse.

THE BOAT COPS used the long hooks, pulled and grappled the stiff body onto a black rubber bag they had spread out on the deck. The man's dark sweatshirt and jacket were waterlogged, soggy, and bunched from the handling.

The blond skipper had a trunk full of crime scene supplies on board and offered plenty of plastic bags to protect evidence.

The deceased, whom Jack suspected might be Chinese—meaning he could fall anywhere from Toishanese to Taiwanese, Cantonese to Shanghainese, or any of a dozen strains of ethnic Chinese—wore dark blue jeans and black Timberland-type boots and looked as generic as anybody in a Gap jeans ad. His jacket had been pulled up by the grappling hook, but just inside the cuff of the left sleeve was a fancy-looking wristwatch. Jack recognized it right away: *a knockoff Rolex*. A Canal Street copy that the Viet-Chinese moved thousands of every year.

Other than the wristwatch, no jewelry.

In his pants pockets, there were forty-four cents, a set of keys on a ring, a red plastic comb. There was a pack of Marlboros in his jacket, along with some soggy scraps of paper. One of the scraps looked like a Chinese receipt for fruit or produce, and the other was a torn piece of a Chinese takeout menu with Chinese numbers and words scribbled across the edges.

The ink on the scraps had started to run.

Jack took tight pictures of everything and then bagged the items, but also considered what *wasn't* there. No wallet, no identification of any kind. No money to speak of, no cell phone, no jewelry. *Maybe the knockoff Rolex had gotten pushed up inside the jacket sleeve and hadn't been noticed.* Except for the wristwatch, Jack suspected it could have been a robbery. The medical examiner would have something more later, Jack knew. *A vic? Or a jumper?* The body hadn't seemed busted up at all, like it'd be if he'd dropped from a great height.

A call came over the sergeant's radio, and they all looked toward Manhattan, where they could see the flashing lights of an EMS unit near the park seawall. The Harbor boat fired up its twin engines as the mate attached the rowboat to its towline.

The river wind gusted up again, and then all Jack could hear was the churning wake and the slapping bounce of the metal rowboat against the waves as they ferried the dead man back toward shore.

Jack scanned the horizon and saw they were past where the Metro-North trains crossed the river and headed north, through the Bronx, Yonkers, and Westchester, to upstate New York.

He wondered where the body had entered the river, but he felt certain it was north, in the vicinity of one of the four bridges spanning the Harlem River. *Statistically, the most common drowning victims are males in their teens through their midtwenties*. Most deceased carried ID or had left a goodbye letter behind. Some had already been reported as missing persons.

Of the annual suicide drownings in New York City, the group didn't amount to more than a dozen or so heartbroken, overwhelmed people on the edge, or mentally ill, over-pressured students and folks caught in scandalous behavior. Unless there was a related catastrophic accident like a plane crash, it wasn't a huge file.

The area bridges over the river now had guardrails and tall fencing along their walkways to deflect potential stunt leapers and suicides, after a spate of them in the 1980s.

The skimming metal sound from the towed rowboat began to slow as they approached the shore.

Smooth and Easy

EMS PLACED THE black body bag on a gurney and took it south to the morgue as a squad car drove Jack and the sergeant six blocks west to the Thirty-Second Precinct. The grittiness of Harlem rolled past until they got to 135th Street.

The Three-Two station house was modern looking, like it had recently gotten a facelift. *Three-two*, Jack remembered— *som yee*—propitious numbers that sounded like the Cantonese for "smooth and easy." At least he was out of the cold, Jack thought, and could deal with the evidence more comfortably.

Sergeant Cohen commandeered a table away from the duty desk where they could review the morning's events. He also provided coffee from the squad's break room.

"Thanks," Jack offered. "I'm also going to need the missing persons reports from the last two days."

"Just the last two?"

"He didn't look like he'd been in the water too long," Jack said. "Let's just see if his profile or picture turns up on the sheet." He knew it was a long shot anyway, and the ME's findings would be hours away.

"Got it," the sergeant agreed, sounding like he'd almost had his fill of overtime. "It may take a little while because of the club fire." Jack thanked him as he went off to the computer room with his coffee.

Jack focused back on the evidence.

THE MUSHY PACK of Marlboros wasn't much of a clue. Missing were two cigarettes, and the pack didn't have any drugs or paraphernalia inside. The pack also didn't have a New York State tax stamp on it, which wasn't very unusual;

untaxed cigarettes poured into New York from neighboring states and from upstate Indian tribes. Given the local hustles, every gang in Chinatown, and every bodega and dive bar, had their fingers in it.

The keys were a mystery: four keys, including one with a rounded, notched cylinder that looked like it belonged to a bike lock. *Was the deceased a takeout-joint deliveryman?* A second key was the type that came in little envelopes, used for safe-deposit boxes at banks. The third key looked normal, like a house key, but the last key looked like the kind you'd find in a pay locker at the bus terminal.

The keys made him think of Ah Por, the old Chinatown wise woman from whom he'd sought clues in previous cases. She could face-read photos and items and provide insights that, eerily, often led to resolutions. Ah Por wasn't clairvoyant, Jack thought. She just had her own touch of yellow Taoist witchcraft.

Pa had gone to her after Ma had passed away, in search of lucky numbers and advice from the *Tong Sing*, the Chinese almanac.

Jack jangled the keys and knew he would bring her his crime scene photos as well. He unzipped the plastic baggies containing the soggy scraps of paper, saw Chinese words at the ends of what appeared to be telephone numbers.

When he punched the numbers through the precinct's computer directory, most of the 888 prefixes belonged to Chinese restaurants and takeout joints in the South Bronx.

The telephone number prefix 888 in Cantonese, *bot bot bot*, sounded like the Chinese word for "luck," times three. Now the use of the 888 prefix could be found on everything from vanity license plates to Asian escort services.

Eight-eight-eight was the most-played number in the Chinese lottery and numbers rackets.

The last two numbers caught his eye. They were both Chinatown numbers, one belonging to the Gee Fraternal and Benevolent Association, and the other to the Dao Foo Wong, or Tofu King.

Inside the wet baggie, the scribbled words continued to run, blend, as he copied them into his notepad.

He called the South Bronx numbers first, found none of them open for business yet. Many takeouts didn't open until 11, figuring that 11 A.M. until 11 P.M. was enough of a dangerous 12-hour day among the *gwai*—the devils, the ghosts.

His call to the Gee Association went to a Cantonese voice message, so he hung up. He'd get a better idea of what connection there was if he visited in person.

He called the Tofu King and asked for Billy Bow. He recognized the voice of the Toishanese counter lady. *"Bee-lee m'mo koy,"* she barked, telling him Billy wasn't there. When he called Billy's cell phone, it went to voice mail: "I'm busy. Leave a message or hang the fuck up." Jack hung up.

He turned back to the evidence on the table. The second wet baggie held another paper scrap with lines across it that made it look like part of a receipt. Jack recognized the Chinese words for "apples," *ping gwo*; "oranges," *chaang gwo*; and "grapes," *poy gee*. "Cherries" was written in English. He wondered about the Chinese fruit and veggie industry. Billy could be of some help with that.

With almost two hours before the Bronx Chinese takeouts opened, he decided to head downtown to Chinatown, where he could get his film processed while he checked out the Gee Association. He'd try Billy Bow at the Tofu King and, with any luck, catch Ah Por at the free morning meal at the Senior Citizens' Center.

Sergeant Cohen made entries into his log, documenting his overtime as he awaited the missing-persons information. Jack felt grateful for the sergeant's help and knew he'd be back to thank him. *Never burn your bridges,* Pa had taught him.

On the way out of the station house, Jack made another call to Billy.

Jouh Chaan Breakfast

BILLY HAD SWITCHED his cell phone to vibrate, like the way he was feeling inside his balls. He refused to be disturbed while he got his hour's worth of flesh from one of the newly arrived whores at Angelina Chao's cathouse on Chrystie Street.

He was enjoying his *jouh chaan,* a breakfast blow job from a big-eyed Thai bar girl just in from Bangkok. He'd covered the earlybird rush at the Tofu King and was now an early bird himself at Angelina's.

Billy preferred to get his pussy rush early, when the flesh was fresh, like just after a shower—clean, pristine—before the Chinatown *hom sup los,* the old horndogs, came around and slopped things up.

On the big bed in Angelina's smaller room, Billy guided the girl onto her back and spread her legs wide. He took a breath and saw himself, all hard and slick and poised to enter her.

He heard his cell vibrating against the chair back where he'd draped his pants.

He ignored it.

Fuck it, he thought, focusing on the fleshy folds that beckoned him.

"God"—he groaned as she slipped him inside her—"damn . . ." In his ecstasy, it was easy to not think about who was calling him.

Short Circuit

JACK CAUGHT A screeching southbound 4 train back to Chinatown.

He'd always taken his disposable plastic cameras to Ah Fook's for processing because he knew Ah Fook had worked as an undertaker in his native Toishan Province, and his family was used to viewing dead bodies. Ah Fook Jr. wouldn't freak out over the usual gruesome or bloody crime scene images that would be printed out from Jack's camera.

He arrived at Ah Fook's 30-Minute Photo just as Ah Fook Jr. was raising the frozen metal roll gate. Jack gave him the plastic camera, promising him *yum ga fear*, coffee, on the return pickup. Junior knew the deal and would process Jack's film first thing.

He continued south on Mott, hoping to check out the Gee Association before dropping by the Tofu King, where he figured Billy would turn up.

At 45 Mott, the Gee Association was nestled in a small building that it owned, with a narrow balcony above a gift shop on the street, one of the few buildings left in Chinatown that still featured a balcony view.

The association was a proud one and was generous with its

donations. Centrally located on Mott Street, the organization was a quiet but effective swing vote in community politics.

The Gees weren't big in New York City like they were in Houston, but to Jack's knowledge the organization never got caught in any scandals or gambling and drug dealing probes. They always stayed under the radar and quietly bought up real estate properties on the Chinatown periphery.

The street door to the association was locked.

Jack pressed the door buttons and waited a minute. Tried it again, waited. There was still no answer, and Jack headed south for the Tofu King when his cell phone sounded.

"What the fuck?" Billy cracked. "You didn't get enough *bean* for one morning?"

"Ha, funny," Jack countered. "Where are you at?"

"Where else?" Billy snapped. "In the shop, twenty-five to life."

"Meet me at Eddie's," Jack said. Eddie's Coffee Shop was on the same block as Ah Fook's 30-Minute Photo.

"Why, *wassup?*"

"I'll fill you in," Jack answered, "but I got a body." He hung up before Billy could ask, *What's it got to do with me?*

JACK GAVE AH Fook Jr. the brown bag of Eddie's *jai fear*, black coffee, and a pair of baked *cha siew baos*, his promised breakfast. Plus a twenty to cover the envelope of photos lying on the counter.

Pictures of the dead.

Jack said, "Say hello to the old man, Fook Senior."

Junior munched on one of the *baos* and grunted his acknowledgment as Jack left.

Outside the photo shop, Jack narrowed his eyes at the

shrill wind knifing through the quiet street and went back down the block toward Eddie's.

Yum Ga Fear

EDDIE'S WAS A hole-in-the-wall coffee shop, frequented by locals and members of the Suey Duck Village Association, which owned the building and was Eddie's landlord.

You rarely saw white people, *lo fan* tourists, in there. Unless they were lost, looking for Edie's Shanghai Soupy Buns, which was on Mulberry, not Mott.

The big plastic Hong Kong–style sign above the storefront façade read EDDIE'S in big letters and COFFEE SHOP in a smaller case. *Cantonese dim sum.* The curved leg of the letter *h* in the word SHOP had broken off, and, having never been repaired, the sign now advertised EDDIE'S COFFEE SLOP.

It didn't seem to matter. The customers who kept the place hopping didn't read English and came for the steamed dumplings; for the box lunches of *lop cheung*, Chinese sausage, and *hom don*, salted egg, for the southern Chinese comfort food they craved.

Inside, Eddie's was just a short diner counter with five stools and a couple of surly waitresses serving the two booths and the four small tables in the back. The baked snacks and main menu orders came out of a dumbwaiter elevator from the basement, where the kitchen ducted out into the back alley, or from the second floor, where they kept two ovens baking *cha siew bao*, braids of raisin bread, and *don tot*, egg custards, sold wholesale to the Filipino and Indonesian mall vendors. Local snack shops snapped up the late-afternoon leftovers.

In the middle, behind the counter, the steam cabinets and twin toaster ovens kept everything hot and moist.

The place was crowded with Chinese men, but Jack picked out Billy right away, seated at one of the small tables in the back. The shop's radio blared out Chinese news of the morning as a waitress brought Billy a pot of tea. Jack came to the table and sat down.

"I ordered some *baos*," Billy said. "You can get whatever."

Jack leaned in across the Formica tabletop, said suspiciously, "I tried calling you earlier, but you weren't in the shop. Nobody knew where—"

"Where *I* was?" Billy asked. "Whaddya, the Chinatown Nazi? I had a construction project, okay?"

"Yeah?" Jack challenged. "Construction, huh? *You?* At eight thirty?"

"Yeah, I was having my pipes cleaned, okay?"

They both laughed before Jack said, "No, seriously, Billy, I got a dead body, and I need to know who and why."

"Well, finding out's the *fun* part, ain't it?" A pause before Billy finished, "And you get *paid* for this?"

The waitress brought the *baos*, departed as they warmed up over the cups of hot tea, both men quiet a moment.

"So we fished this body out of the Harlem River," Jack began.

"Nobody I know, I hope," said Billy.

"There was no ID, no driver's license, green card, nothing."

"So he's a John Doe?"

"He was Asian," Jack added.

"Okay, a John *Cho?*" Billy chuckled. "A John *Ho?*"

Not funny, Jack said with his eyes.

"Okay," Billy said. "Let's get this again. This dead guy? What's he got to do with me?"

Jack showed him the baggie with the takeout-scrap list of numbers.

"He carried a list of business numbers, and one of them was yours."

"*Mine?*" Billy sounded truly shocked.

"Actually for the Tofu King."

"What? He died from eating bad tofu?" Billy stiffened.

"Come on, Billy . . ."

"What?" Billy repeated. "Anyone can have the shop's number! They walk in, grab a business card. We run an ad in the Chinese press, *Mon Bo* and *Sai Gai*. We got flyers we're handing out." He shook his head. "What the fuck kinda clue is that anyway?"

"You can't think of why he'd have the shop's number?"

"He wanted to buy some tofu?" Billy shrugged.

Jack paused, took a breath, drained the tea with a frown.

"Anybody can call, place an order," muttered Billy defensively.

"This doesn't feel like a takeout order," Jack said, cold as stone.

"I don't allow personal calls. But maybe there's an emergency, who knows? Someone looking for a relative. Or a job. Who knows? What, I gotta monitor phone calls now?"

Jack showed Billy one of the headshots hot out of Ah Fook's.

"You ever seen this guy?" Jack asked.

"Never," Billy answered with certainty. "Too bad, but homeboy looks at peace."

"The second number on that scrap menu belongs to the Gee Association. Maybe he was a member or an associate?"

Billy checked the wall clock. "The association? Those *jooks* ain't there before eleven, man. They make up for it by opening early on weekends, when more seniors need services." He chomped down his *bao*. "We got five minutes."

"'We'?"

"I know the super there. They call him the English secretary, but he does some of the janitorial work. And the Gees order a lot of bean from me."

Jack slipped a five under the teapot and finished his *bao*. Steam poured out of the counter cabinets, fogging up the room. He knew Billy'd be good for something.

Gee Whiz

THEY CAME TO the street door on Mott, and Billy pulled it open without hesitation. He held it for Jack, who stepped inside, quietly impressed. They went up to the second floor, where two of the front apartments had been converted to an office and an open area that the association could use for meetings, meals, and mah-jongg games. Simple bench seating lined the two long walls. There were two racks of metal chairs and a line of card tables folded against the back wall. A few old black-and-white photos of the Gees' village in China, including a group shot of the revered founding Gee elders, hung across the top of the main walls.

There was an altar table in the far corner, near a back window.

The man behind the desk in the office area looked to be in his fifties, mostly bald except for a few long strands of hair, which he had combed over across the top of his head. His attention was on the lid of the container of Chinese coffee on the desk, opening it without causing a spill.

He was surprised to look up and see Billy.

"Ah Gee *doy*!" Billy grinned, patting him across the shoulder. *Gee boy!* in his best Toishanese drawl.

"*Dofu doy*!" The man grinned back, putting the steamy cup aside. *Tofu boy!* he said, turning his gaze to include Jack.

"*Ngo pong yew*," Billy introduced Jack. "He's my friend." It wasn't a shake-hands moment, and both men nodded respectfully. Then Billy added, "*Chaai lo*, he's a cop."

The grin left the man's face slowly as Jack flapped open his jacket and flashed his gold badge and, inadvertently, also the pistol butt sticking out of his waistband holster.

"And he has some questions," Billy continued, "maybe you can help him with."

"Of course," the man answered, his mouth small now. "*If I can . . .*"

"Who answers the phone here?" Jack asked casually.

"Whoever sits here," the man answered. "Sometimes the vice president, but mostly me. If I go to lunch or step away on other duties, then any member can answer and take a message. It's usually about banquet arrangements or funerals. Or group trips to the cemeteries."

Jack placed the plastic-bagged menu scrap on the desk. The man looked over the telephone numbers with the 888 prefixes diligently.

"Those numbers mean anything to you?" Jack asked.

"Not really, no." There was caution in the man's voice now.

"Not familiar numbers?"

"No." He took a sip from the container of coffee.

"Lucky Dragon? Lucky Phoenix?" Jack continued, "Any of these sound familiar? How about China Village? Or Golden City?"

"They sound like Chinese restaurants," the man offered.

Jack asked, "Any idea why your association's telephone number is grouped with those restaurants' numbers?"

"I have no idea." But his face told a different story as the man began to back up, reconsidering a bigger involvement than he'd bargained for. He glanced at Billy, who remained intensely quiet during Jack's interview. Billy, sitting in the catbird seat, offering no relief.

Jack pressed, "Can I speak with the vice president? Or the president?"

There was a pause as the man's eyes left Billy and drifted back to the plastic baggie. He took another sip of coffee, enjoying it less now.

"The president and the vice president are overseas," he said, almost confidentially. "But they wouldn't be involved in the day-to-day operations anyway. The positions are only ceremonial. Unofficially, I'm the English secretary, but I don't receive all the calls."

"And you don't log the calls?"

"Who keeps a record of calls, anyway, these days? Only the phone company. And that's because they want to bill you."

Jack placed the second baggie on the desk, showing the produce receipt from the body. "Does this look familiar?" he asked.

"No," the man said firmly after only a glance. "It looks like fruit."

Jack put the headshot of the deceased on the desk, next to the man's container of coffee. "Ever see this man?" Jack quietly asked.

"No" was his answer, his eyes dancing but lingering longer this time. "Sorry." The face of death had turned him off, clammed him up, and Billy exchanged looks with Jack. Billy was a face of disappointment, and Jack couldn't mask his doubt.

"*M'hou yisee*, hah?" the man said regretfully. "Sorry that my answers are no help." Clenched in his face, clearly, was his reluctance to say anything that in any way represented the voice of the association. He didn't want to involve the group in any outside trouble. He didn't want to go anywhere near the dead face in the photo, but the phone numbers seemed to make him hesitate before backing off.

The man looked at Billy for a long moment. *Bee-lee* boy was Bow Ying's son, he knew, an upcoming young businessman and heir to the tofu throne, but in their little Chinatown world, Billy didn't carry any more weight than that. It was only business after all, but bringing a cop around was an awkward surprise.

Jack offered one of his NYPD detective's cards. "Please call me if anything occurs to you."

The man nodded politely and accepted the card.

Billy bluntly broke the ice with an unrelated question: · "So you have enough tofu for Chin's wedding banquet?"

Frozen momentarily by the change in direction, the man answered, "I'll call you."

Jack thanked him, and they left the room, leaving him in peace with his morning coffee.

OUT ON MOTT Street it was starting to snow, with big flakes of white slowly covering the icy gray debris on the ground. Billy fired up a cigarette and took a long drag.

"Bullshit. What a waste of time."

"Relax," Billy said. "The man got uptight. Your badge, the gun, the dead man's picture. Hey, it's easier to just know nothing."

Jack knew it as Chinese truth, centuries of perfecting this type of *cooperation* with the authorities, where no one ever implicates himself. *See no evil. Hear no evil. Speak no evil.*

"He didn't see you as *Chinese*, Jacky boy," Billy continued. "The only thing yellow about you was your badge. That stinkin' badge, my brother, sometimes opens doors, but sometimes closes them, too."

They continued toward the Tofu King.

Billy concluded, "The man doesn't trust what might happen to his words once they leave his mouth and slide into your cop's ear. Ya dig?"

Jack frowned as he checked his watch. "Just let me know if you hear anything." He left Billy at the tofu shop, made a left onto Bayard, and headed toward the Senior Citizens' Center. The falling flakes, he knew, would drive the elderly indoors to the free hot congee breakfast provided by the center.

He hoped the old woman, Ah Por, would be there.

THE SENIOR CENTER occupied the first floor, including the old cafeteria, of what used to be Public School 23.

What was once an elementary-school lunchroom was now used to cook and serve meals to 300 elderly Chinese—hot *congee* in the winter, tofu dishes and melon soups in the summer, plates of rice with sides of Chinese greens, *choy*, and fruit.

A cup of tea was always available for the asking.

The temperature rose noticeably as Jack stepped into the lunchroom, a humid mass of gray heads, warming in their down-filled jackets and quilted *meen ngaap* vests. He could hear Chinese Wah Fow radio over the PA system, barely audible over the din of chattering voices and clashing metal from the kitchen area.

He looked toward Ah Por's usual spot, near the big window facing the back courtyard. It was crowded there, and he couldn't tell for sure with all the puffy, shapeless clothes, so he moved in for a closer look.

The sea of bodies fluidly parted for Jack, a young stranger, and rejoined in his wake. Jack could feel the looks of curiosity following him.

He found Ah Por alone at the end of one of the bench tables near the back exit. There was an empty bowl next to her, and she was watching an old Hong Kong movie playing on one of the overhead TV monitors.

Jack took a seat opposite her and caught her attention by touching the back of the veiny hand she'd rested on the table. "Ah Por," he acknowledged quietly.

She stared at him curiously, smiling, as he bowed slightly.

"Ah doy," she said, using his boyhood tag. *Onset dementia*, Jack thought, before she added, "You *are* your father's son." She hesitated a moment when Jack pressed the folded five-dollar bill into her hand.

"What *now*, this time?" she asked, a quiet sadness in her eyes.

He took out the plastic-bagged scraps of evidence first, slipped them onto the table in front of her.

"These numbers mean anything?" Jack asked.

"The plastic blocks my old fingers."

Jack unzipped the baggies, allowed her to touch the damp scraps of paper with her fingertips. Her breathing got shallower as she lightly ran her fingers over the phone numbers, over the Chinese words on the produce receipt.

"The numbers are looking for money," she said, "*won cheen.*" *Won cheen* also meant "looking for work," Jack knew. Or it could mean "collecting on a debt."

"There is a *dai lo baan*," she added, falling into a breathy exclaiming cadence. A *big boss?* wondered Jack. *Organized crime or Bruce Lee movies?* There was a pause, and Ah Por glanced up at the TV monitor, distracted.

He quickly slipped her another folded five, took the baggies back, and passed her the keys.

She took a couple of long breaths, feeling the cuts and edges of the different keys.

"There is a very small closet," she began. A *locker, storage*, Jack thought.

"*Bo, see,*" she added. *Precious* and *a key?* Jack wondered. *A safe, or safe deposit?*

"*Mo yung,*" she said as she flipped another key. "Useless." *Its use had expired? A transient key, a changed lock cylinder?*

She handed back the keys as Jack slipped her one of the snapshots of the deceased. A face reading. She held the photo with both hands, seeing the river-wet face with dripping hair falling back from it, caressing the image of the dead man with her thumbs, murmuring like she was comforting a grandchild with a fever. *Don't worry. It was all just a nightmare, this journey to the West.*

"What?" Jack wondered aloud.

"North," she said. "He came from the north." *Yeah, north Manhattan*, Jack remembered. *Maybe the Bronx? Or even farther north? The routes of human smugglers.*

"He's always moving," she continued. *Immigrants on the move? Like migrant workers?* he pondered. *Or moving, like on a bike? A deliveryman? A student with a part-time job?*

Ah Por closed her eyes, switched to the Toishanese dialect, saying, "Money is the root of all evil." She placed the snapshot gently on the table and pushed it back to Jack. He took a moment to absorb her last statement before giving her the five-dollar tip he had ready. *The root of all evil.*

She pocketed the five and smiled, dismissing Jack with a wave of her gnarled hand. She resumed watching the Hong Kong movie as if Jack had never been there. He knew it was a wrap, finished, gave her a small bow, and left the table.

He went back through the elderly crowd toward the front door, where the winter wind seeped in and reminded him of death in the cold and uncaring city.

Outside, the day was still steel gray as the wind had blown itself out.

North, Jack was thinking, Ah Por's word.

He dropped down to the Brooklyn Bridge station and caught another subway northbound, with the South Bronx addresses rattling like dice in his head. He was seeing snake eyes, but what was clear to him: a dead Asian with forty-four cents in his pockets had put him on this 4 train to visit four Chinese restaurants, all situated in the confines of the

Forty-Fourth Precinct. He didn't like the way the numbers lined up, *four* being the number that the Chinese hated the most, *say* in Cantonese, sounding phonetically like *death*. In this case, death times six.

He heard Ah Por's words of yellow witchcraft in his head. Not that he was superstitious, just wary of what destiny might hold.

The train rattled, rumbled its way out of Manhattan.

The restaurant locations clustered around the subway lines, with the Lexington and the West Side lines pushing across the Harlem River to the mean ghetto streets of High-bridge, Tremont, Morrisania, where the immigrant Chinese restaurants served and delivered to the *gwai lo* devils at their own peril. Hard and bitter mining, *ngai phoo*, eking out a living in the *gum shan*, in the mountains of gold.

A bleak ghettoscape flashed by outside the train windows as the subway emerged aboveground. *Always moving*, he heard Ah Por saying inside his head.

Speak No Evil

BILLY LOOKED UP from the steamy *foo jook* bean sticks as the English secretary entered the Tofu King.

"*Du mort yah?*" Billy asked, working his slang Toishanese. "What? Add something to the Chin order?"

The secretary glanced around, nodded toward a back room. "Let's talk in your office," he said.

"Sure," Billy said, pulling off the sanitary plastic gloves. It was how they usually tallied their tofu orders. They went into the small makeshift office, and Billy closed the door.

"What's up?" Billy asked, turning to see the man reaching into his coat. The motion froze Billy momentarily, made him think of his gun in the desk drawer. But what came out of the coat was a fresh pint bottle of Johnnie Walker Black, which he placed on the desk.

"About your *chaai lo* police friend," the secretary started with a frown. Billy put two clean shot glasses on the desk, and they sat down.

"You weren't much help." Billy smiled disarmingly. The man snap-twisted off the cap and pushed the bottle toward Billy.

"Those restaurants belong to Jook Mun Gee," the secretary began. "And I don't want to go near *whatever* this is."

"Jook Mun Gee?" Billy said, interest piqued.

"Correct."

Billy poured two big shots from the small bottle.

"And I can't involve the association," the man continued.

Billy raised his glass, said, "I understand completely."

They clinked, and each threw back a full swallow.

"Off the record," Billy said as he refilled their glasses. "My cop friend." He toasted. "He'll appreciate the favor."

Backtrack

JACK GOT OFF at Mount Eden and decided to check out the two restaurants closer to the West Side lines, then work his way back farther west to the river, where the other two restaurants were. The takeouts' addresses appeared to be at least six city blocks apart, as if they'd agreed to keep the spacing fair and even, not be too close so as to eat out of each other's golden rice bowl.

The only people on the streets looked die-hard ghetto, sullen, but the two "Lucky" restaurants weren't too far off the beaten track of burned-out tenements, graffitied, abandoned buildings, and vacant lots.

The first place, Lucky Dragon on West Tremont, was just a hole-in-the-wall fast-food takeout joint. The shop looked worn down, neglected, like it'd had a hard-luck history. *Hopeful immigrants looking for their piece of the American Dream*, thought Jack.

There were no customers, and Jack wondered if they'd just opened for the day.

He didn't see a delivery bike anywhere, but inside it was a typical mom-and-pop takeout counter with no seating. You bought food like it was a ghetto liquor store: cash went into a teller's slot, where a girl took your order and made change. The eggroll specials came out from behind the Plexiglas, boxed and bagged to go. No hanging around.

Protocols of the streets ruled, Jack knew, like the dealers on the corners.

Cop and go, yo. Don't be lingering at this motherfucka . . .

No problema, hombre. Buy and blow.

No troubles, man. Five-oh on the roll.

Farther behind the Plexiglas was a fast-food kitchenette where a middle-aged Chinese husband-and-wife team was firing up the dark woks and preparing soups and side dishes for the lunch special rush. *Fried rice, eggroll, and a discount can of no-name soda: $2.99. No delively.*

Jack badged the cashier girl, who called out to the man at the wok, who turned and looked at Jack a long moment before waving him in. The girl pressed a buzzer until he went through a notch at the end of the counter.

"*Ni yao shen me?*" he asked Jack, working the oily ladle. "What do you want?" *Mandarin*, thought Jack, *but with a Fukienese accent*. The wife watched them, stirring a pot of simmering wonton broth as Jack showed the man the photo of the deceased.

"Know this person?" Jack asked in his clipped Mandarin. The man glanced at the snapshot, shook his head, and, without missing a beat swirling the ladle, answered, "*Wo bu zhidao,*" *I don't know*, as Jack showed him the menu scrap with the phone numbers.

"*Bu zhidao,*" the man repeated as he seasoned the oil. Jack took a paper takeout menu from the counter, saw that it wasn't a match.

"*Wo tai mangle.*" The man shrugged apologetically. *I'm too busy, don't know nothing.*

Was it the typical Chinese reluctance to get involved again?

The front door opened, and two homeless-looking *Boricuas* staggered in, jangling fistfuls of filthy coins. Jack felt he was wasting time and got a sympathetic look from the wife as she slid two eggrolls into the hot oil.

He thanked them on the way out, passed the men who smelled like rum and stale pot. When he looked back, the cashier girl was counting the greasy pile of coins in the slot, a horrified smile on her face.

THE LUCKY PHOENIX was six blocks back through the gloom. Jack felt his luck needed to change and hoped the Phoenix would turn things around. Halfway there, he saw the neighborhood change ever so slightly; the streets seemed cleaner, and some of the Depression-era buildings had survived neglect and abuse.

The Lucky Phoenix had a larger storefront than Lucky Dragon, with two small square tables against one wall and a window counter where customers could snack standing up. No Plexiglas except where it partitioned off the kitchen area.

There was a bike locked to the window-gate rail.

Jack tried the cylindrical key on the lock but got no fit.

Inside were four customers eating, and a flurry of phone orders added to the brisk business scene. Jack took one of the paper menus from a wall rack and compared it with the evidence scrap.

A perfect match, printwise, of the menu format. Jack felt his luck changing but waited for a break before quietly badging the counterman. The man yelled into the partitioned kitchen, and a manager type came out, a harried-looking Chinese man with an order pad in his hand. He saw Jack's badge and motioned him over to a rear door open to a back alley.

They stood there as Jack took out the photo while the man lit up a cigarette.

"Seen him before?" Jack asked in quiet Cantonese.

The manager took a long look over three drags on the butt.

"Resembles someone," he said finally, "who came looking for work. But we had enough help. He was friendly. Name was *Zhang*, I think."

Chang in Cantonese, Jack knew, became *Zhang* with those coming out of China, but the written character for both names was the same in Chinese:

張

"When was this?" Jack asked.

"It was still warm then. September. Maybe October." *Four months ago*, but at least he'd picked up the trail, thought Jack.

"Where'd he go after?"

"*Boo ji dao*," the man said with a smile and a shrug. *I don't know* with a Hong Kong accent.

Jack thanked him and followed the trail west into the Highbridge section. He looked around for a cab or bus but saw none and kept walking. The other two restaurants were close to University Avenue, almost a mile away.

He moved at a brisk pace through the cold.

The numbers are looking for money, Ah Por had said. Jack now knew the deceased *Zhang* had been looking for work and was calling these restaurants. *But this was four months ago?*

After marching several blocks, he came to an intersection where a blue-and-white patrol car had stopped for a light. Jack caught the shotgun-seat sergeant's eye and badged him. The passenger window was powered down.

"Hey, Sarge," Jack said like they were friends. "I'm working a John Doe. How about a lift to University Avenue?"

The white sergeant, with a salt-and-pepper crew cut, took a full ten seconds to digest Jack's presence—the first *Oriental* cop he'd ever encountered—quietly stunned by Jack's perfect New *Yawk* accent.

"Get in," the sarge growled.

Jack slid into the backseat, caught his breath as the uniformed driver gunned the Ford toward University.

"What precinct *you?*" the sarge asked, craning his neck back to get an eye-corner glimpse of Jack.

Jack heard it *Yu*, like they really knew each other. *Brothers. Blood brothers. NYPD-blue blood brothers.*

"Down in the Ninth," Jack answered.

"Where'd you find the stiff?" asked the sarge.

"He was a floater," Jack said as pockets of gentrified streets flashed by.

"No shit. Was that the Harlem River thing this morning?"

"You got it."

"I heard it over the radio," the sarge continued. "And they brought you up from the Lower East Side?"

Jack nodded *yeah* at the crew cut, studying him now in the rearview mirror. *You got it.* A patrol squawk over the radio broke the long silence as they approached University.

"Why you?" the sarge finally asked. Jack paused before answering, tempted to say, *Because I'm Chinese?*

"Maybe all the dicks are busy with the club fire?" Jack answered instead.

"Probably that." The sarge grunted in agreement as Jack hopped out on University.

"Thanks for the ride, Sarge." Jack pumped a thumbs-up.

The sarge returned Jack a *whatever* salute as the blue-and-white sped off toward the Washington Bridge. Jack took a breath and turned back down the South Bronx streets, looking for any sign of a Golden City.

ACCORDING TO THE map, Golden City was closer to the Harlem River and the creeping pockets of gentrification, so the restaurant's owners could expect a lucrative takeout and delivery business. But closer to the river also meant closer to the Morris Houses, the notorious projects known for breeding stone-cold teenagers looking to get rich quick or die trying.

Jack knew that gangster turf wars and drug dealing in the projects accounted for a big chunk of the Forty-Fourth Precinct's crime stats. As he walked into the river wind, he looked for delivery bikes on the street but saw none. *Rolling on deliveries*, he figured.

He got to the restaurant address quickly, the location bearing such little signage that he almost walked past it. Golden City reminded him of a Chinatown restaurant, with five red booths in a line against a long wall and three small tables opposite them. There were a couple of gold fan wall decorations, and GUM GWOK LOY (Gold City Come) was written in big, gold Chinese characters

The place was half full. He saw that the kitchen was in the back, the kind you could *hear* more than see, with the clatter and salty talk from the chefs and the *da jops*, kitchen help, the noise carrying through to the other side of the pass-through, where the waiters hung out for the pickup bell.

There was a cashier station beside the front entrance, with a register behind a plastic divider displaying a Bronx tour map and a Yankees calendar. There were photographs of local sports teams covering the area where the cashier, a Chinese girl who looked like she was in high school, was taking receipts and making change with a smile.

"*Ging lay*," Jack requested. "I need the manager."

She tapped a *ding* out of the takeout bell, and a man in black near the kitchen looked up as she waved him over.

Jack met him halfway and badged him into one of the empty booths.

"Know him?" Jack asked, laying the photo on the table.

The manager took a long look at the snapshot before replying "*Jun Wah*" in Hong Kong Cantonese.

"He worked here?"

The man nodded *yes*, pushing the photo back.

"Last name?"

"Chang, or Zhang. *Jun Wah Zhang.* What happened to him?"

"We think he drowned."

"He worked here for about a month," the man continued. "Then he quit."

"What was his job?" Jack pressed.

"Deliveries, mostly."

"What about when it's slow?"

The question seemed to surprise the manager. "General cleaning. Helping in the kitchen, sometimes washing dishes." It sounded to Jack like they got every minute's worth of muscle, wrung every ounce of sweat, out of the dead man. Chang. *Jun Wah.*

The manager was glib, using quick-talking Hong Kong slang, coolly moving the conversation along like he was dancing around the dead body, not wanting to dirty his shoes.

Jack asked, "Got an address for him?"

"*M'jidou.*" He shook his head. "No idea."

"Why did he quit?" Jack continued. *Because you were working him to death?*

"He wasn't happy with the money." The manager's tone implied *ingrate.*

"When did he quit?"

"It was November sometime, around Thanksgiving."

"Did he seem depressed?" Jack held up the photo again. "He mention any problems?"

"*M'jidou*." The man shrugged. "No idea. He kept to himself. Did his job, took his tips, and left."

No human resources needed, thought Jack.

A group of postal workers entered the restaurant and was greeted by the cashier. Jack eyed the three other restaurant workers. Two waiters and a kitchen helper in a soiled white apron.

"He wanted more money," the manager offered as he shifted his attention between Jack and the new customers. "What can you do?" He caught Jack's interest in the workers: "They're just part-timers. And they're new. They just started a month ago. Fresh off the boat." That smooth Hong Kong–nese again. *So they wouldn't have known him.*

Jack accepted the personnel turnover angle, especially up here in the Bronx, and he knew that bosses liked part-timers who could work off the books, who didn't require insurance, and from whom they could extract a portion of their tips. The *da jop* looked like he was working his way through a five-year indentured servitude, and the cashier was probably one of the boss's schoolgirl nieces.

Ding!

"Sorry." The manager rose from the booth. "It's *chaan kay*, the lunch rush." He went to greet and seat the postal workers in his most obsequious manner as one of the waiters readied a pot of tea.

Savory steam leaked out near the swinging kitchen door as Jack slipped out of the booth. He felt he'd gotten enough for the meantime and knew he could always come back if necessary.

Turning up his collar, he went back out into the street, wondering what else he'd find when he got to the China Village.

IT WAS ANOTHER five-block march toward the river, and along the way Jack noticed condominium developments alongside rehabilitated prewar buildings. He half expected to see a deliveryman ride past and jiggled Chang's bike key in his pocket.

The sign above a big picture-window front read CHINA VILLAGE in an Oriental font, braced on both sides by stencils of bamboo plants. Jack looked inside through the picture window, saw two big, empty round tables in the middle of the dining floor. Track lighting gave the setting a soft touch, like a theater set. Farther back, the booths and the small tables were all occupied, diners watching the big-screen TV on the back wall. A Knicks recap. The menu in the window offered bottled beer and charged an uncorking fee if you brought your own wine. Yankees and Giants posters hung just inside the entrance, giving the place a New York sports vibe.

China Village probably didn't get a lot of *turistas* in the South Bronx, Jack knew, but the park waterfront and Yankee Stadium still attracted people to the general area. Maybe the restaurant attracted sports fans who wanted a quick, tasty meal on the cheap and a beer or two before the big game or match.

Jack's focus came back to the front. Again, the Yankees championship team photo and the Knicks calendar at a cashier's station by the wall near the main door. He imagined the dinner rush was probably better than the lunch crowd and wondered if people here wagered on sports events. And *who* might be handling the action.

Inside were two waiters and a cashier lady. He spotted a manager type who looked strangely similar to the one at Golden City. *Maybe it was the all-black outfits?*

Jack backed away from the window, drew a long cold *shaolin* breath, and closed his eyes. Trying to pull together the clues, the missing pieces.

When he opened his eyes, he saw what he'd been looking for—a Chinese deliveryman on a bike, pedaling quickly and empty-handed toward the China Village. *Looks like a student,* Jack thought, before badging the bike man over. The guy was probably in his twenties but looked younger, wearing a suspicious, wary look on his face.

"*Dailo ah,*" Jack addressed him in street Cantonese, giving the man *face* and putting him at ease. "You could be a big help, brother."

"*Mot'si ah sir?*" the deliveryman answered respectfully in slang Cantonese. "What's the problem?"

"Seen this man?" Jack asked as he held up the snapshot of Chang. Recognition and shock crossed the man's face.

"*Wah!*" he said. "*Gowsing gum yeung ah?*"

Wow, was what Jack heard, *he's come to this?*

"He worked here?" Jack followed. "What's his name?"

"Singarette," the man said softly, catching his breath. He smiled sadly and shook his head.

"Singarette?" Jack pressed.

"His name is Sing, but we called him Singarette." He looked away from the photo. "What happened to him?"

"He was in the river," Jack answered, holding up the photo again. "Why Singarette?"

"He was generous with cigarettes. Always offering during the smoke breaks. The men would say, 'Here comes Singarette!' And he'd light you up, too, flicking his lighter."

"His lighter?"

"One of those Vietnam War lighters. Metal. Had a war eagle on it. He could whip up a flame with just a flick of his thumb." There was a pause as he looked around before continuing. "I don't want to get into any trouble talking to you. Let me get the bike into the alley, and I'll call it a cigarette break."

They went into an alley next to the restaurant, and Jack could see that the man's bike lock and chain wouldn't match up with the cylindrical key in his pocket. *But there had been no lighter on the body. Had it fallen out somewhere, maybe in the river? Along with his ID and his money?*

The man lit up a cigarette, offered one to Jack.

He declined. "What was his job here?"

"Like me. Deliveries," the man said, answering between puffs.

"Only deliveries?"

"Well, they let him wait tables for one shift, but he wasn't happy with that."

"Unhappy? Why's that?"

"They gave him one day a week off deliveries because he'd gotten robbed. He was nervous about deliveries."

"What about the robbery?"

"We've all been robbed. Some got hurt." He drew deep on the cigarette. "He didn't like delivering to the projects. And he'd been robbed before, at his last job."

"And where was that?"

"Gum Gwok, not far from here." The Golden City was still fresh in Jack's mind.

"Did he seem depressed?" Jack asked. "Or angry?"

"He was mad that the restaurant wouldn't cover his losses from the mugging."

"From working at Gum Gwok or here?" Jack continued.

"Both, I guess. He was angry with them all. They didn't even offer him back what they took out of his tips. Then he quit."

"When was this?" asked Jack, trying to get a read on the dead man's recent frame of mind.

"It was in January. After Chinese New Year."

"Know where he went?"

"No idea."

The noisy clatter of kitchen work from inside the rear door interrupted them for a moment. "Do you know where he was from?"

"Not sure. He said he'd been a student, but needed to work and hoped to get something in Chinatown."

"Why Chinatown?"

"He said his village association was there, and maybe they would help." He worked his cigarette almost to the end. *The Gee Association*, Jack suspected, knew more than it was telling.

"What happened with the robberies?"

"You mean the police? Sing didn't go. Said it was useless. A waste of time. He'd only lose another day's pay."

"So he didn't report it?"

The man shook his head *no* as he finished his cigarette. "I don't think so." He answered Jack's frown, saying, "I got robbed once. At knifepoint. Three guys against me, on a bike. The bosses didn't help, but I reported it."

"And what happened?" Jack asked.

"I went into the station and looked at photographs. But it happened at night. It was dark. They all wore hoodies, and they all looked about the same. I remembered the *knives* more than the faces, and I couldn't pick out anyone for sure."

"It's good that you reported it," Jack advised. "At least the cops know about it, could look out for crime like that."

The man didn't look convinced, changed the subject. "I lost two hundred dollars," he said bitterly.

Jack redirected the talk. "Where did he live, this brother, Singarette?"

"*Mox-say-go*," he said, grinning. "He was joking that he was living with Mexicans."

"Mexicans?" *Bronx immigrants from Mexico?*

"Maybe one of Gooba Jai's places."

Gooba Jai was *Chino-Cubano*, one of the later waves of Chinese-Cuban immigrants who found their Spanish-speaking way to the South Bronx and bought blighted buildings in decaying neighborhoods, properties no one else wanted. Those derelict, rent-controlled tenements were set up as rent-a-bed deals for Chinese and Latino workers or visitors to the Bronx.

"I don't know any addresses," he said.

"Did he have any other problems?" Jack pressed. "Girlfriend? School?"

"No. But he mentioned a gambling situation, had to do with him getting robbed. Like he was trying to win back what he'd lost."

"Gambling?" challenged Jack. "Up here? Where?"

"Don't know, but everyone talks about Fay Lo's."

"*Fay Lo?*" Fat boy. "Where?"

Jack got the *don't know* shrug again, just as the China Village manager that Jack had spotted earlier came out of the front door and peered into the alley.

"*DEW NA MA GA HEI!*" he cursed in Toishanese as he spotted the deliveryman. *Motherfucker! Your deliveries are getting cold!*

Jack handed the man his detective's card as he started moving his bike toward the front. He gave Jack a departing nod.

"Call me if you think of anything else," Jack called out after him.

The manager cast a quick look in Jack's direction and was momentarily puzzled. Then he shivered in the cold and ran back inside the China Village. Jack imagined him to be as glib as the manager of the Golden City, tactful, expeditious, but not very helpful. They volunteered nothing and spoke like they'd been pre-lawyered up.

Jack couldn't recall much else on the Chinese-Cubans in the Bronx, but he felt like he'd struck a vein. He was pondering *Mexicano Chino-Cubano* crash pads and Fay Lo's gambling operations when his cell phone jumped around in his jacket pocket.

He tapped up a number he didn't recognize, but the phone voice belonged to Sergeant Cohen from the Three-Two.

"The report's in," he advised. "Report to the morgue, ASAP."

ON THE WAY downtown, Jack tried to put together what he'd gathered. The dead man was a deliveryman/waiter/student named Chang, who'd been robbed and had a gambling problem. He'd been angry, maybe depressed. Maybe suicidal. The jumper/floater scenario was unreeling in his head.

He arrived at Manhattan's West Side before he knew it.

Steel Cold Dead

HE STOOD IN the cold, stainless-steel stillness of the room, its wall of metal doors housing the dead, the afterworld rendition of a Fukienese rent-a-bed. A female morgue assistant handed him the certificate of death. She said, "Dr. Jacobson will be right back," before walking away.

Jack scanned the certificate. The decedent, John Doe, was listed as Asian. Under the section "COD," the entry for cause of death stunned him: *Sharp force piercing through heart.* Manner of death: HOMICIDE.

But how? There'd been no blood and no visible trauma or defensive wounds. He imagined the frozen body in the frozen river again, was turning the image over in his head, when the medical examiner appeared. He looked like an Ivy League professor in a gray smock.

"A stab in the heart, Doctor?" Jack asked incredulously. "I didn't see any blood."

"It was easy to miss, Detective. A single thrust. A very thin wound." Jacobson lifted a black hoodie sweatshirt, still wet, from one of the gurneys and held it open. He indicated a thin slit in the fabric where a sharp force had penetrated. "The sweatshirt and undershirt, everything was wet and black and bunched up. We didn't see the wound until we got the clothes off."

"But no blood?" Jack repeated.

"It's possible, from floating in the cold water for hours," the doctor suggested, "that any blood could have washed out. And it's also harder to see blood on black." He opened one of the metal drawers and slid out a rack with the decedent's autopsied corpse. *Chang,* thought Jack. *Jun Wah, aka Singarette. It comes down to a body on the slab at the morgue.* A Y-cut where they'd opened him up ran from chest to navel, but what caught Jack's eye was the single wound over the heart area, a thin vertical slit barely an inch tall, with matching bruises at either end.

"The skin normally contracts around the wound," Jacobson said, "but the cold river water could have helped close it. But we can tell that it was a double-edged weapon, which is unusual."

"Like a sword?" Jack asked.

"More like a *dirk.*"

Jack narrowed his eyes at the wound, trying to imagine the weapon. Like a Greek or Roman dagger, the kind you'd see in a knife collector's mail-order catalog.

"Or a dagger," the doctor continued. "In this case a short dagger, maybe a four-and-a-half-inch blade. See the rounded abrasions at either end of the cut? The dagger had a hand-guard. It pierced his heart but not through to his back. Severed the aorta and the veins around it."

"It was driven in to the hilt then?" Jack said.

"With tremendous force. That's what caused the hand-guard marks."

Driven forward and held until the man was dead, the weapon could kill in less than three minutes.

"Given the angle of the thrust, I'd say it was a left-handed person, someone taller than the decedent. Maybe five foot ten inches, almost like yourself."

"I don't see any defensive wounds," Jack said. "And you said only through the sweatshirt and undershirt, but not the jacket? So the jacket was open?"

"Yes."

"So he never saw it coming?" Jack said as he gained clarity.

"We don't know that."

"He let his guard down. Or it was someone he knew."

"That's for *you* to find out, Detective, isn't it?" Jacobson smiled faintly. He took from the gurney the knockoff Rolex that Chang had been wearing, laid it next to the corpse. It had stopped at 10:30 P.M.

"Estimated time of death is between nine thirty and ten P.M.," Jacobson continued. "The casing and the metal clock mechanism freeze in the water and contract and slow to a stop. Within an hour or two."

"Think he was dead before he hit the water?" Jack asked.

"Very possible," Jacobson answered. "Or close to it. There wasn't much water in his lungs." He bagged the watch and gave it to Jack.

Ah Por, thought Jack. He'd want her to get a touch on the watch before it went into the crime lab. Maybe they'd get some prints off it. He took a last look at the corpse before Jacobson pushed the drawer back in.

"Good luck, Detective," Jacobson said as he moved to the next body.

Jack thanked him and left the room of the dead.

Outside, the cold, crisp air revived him. His cell jangled with a familiar number.

"Find out anything, *bro*?" It was Billy Bow.

"Yeah, he's Chinese," snapped Jack. "Why?"

"Last name Chang, right?" teased Billy.

"And you know that *how*?" Jack countered.

"Ancient Chinese secret."

"Stop fucking around, Billy. It's a homicide deal now."

"Meet me at Grampa's."

"What the fuck?" Jack started.

But Billy had hung up.

Golden Star

THE GOLDEN STAR Bar and Grill, also known as Grampa's, was a revered Chinatown jukebox joint. Located on the far stretch of East Broadway, the hot spot was a big dugout basement three steps down from the street, far enough away from the core of Chinatown to escape the influence of the traditional old-line *tongs*.

Because Grampa's mixed bag of Lower East Side regulars included Chinatown denizens, blacks and Latinos from the projects, and rotating teams of undercover cops, the popular bar was considered neutral turf even for the rival street gangs that rolled in and out. Hardheads looking for a beef usually took their differences down the street beneath the Manhattan Bridge or under the highway by the East River.

Inside, under dim blue lighting, a long, oval-shaped bar dominated the space. There was an arcade bowling game up front, a big jukebox set up in the middle, and a pool table in the back next to the kitchen.

Grampa's was almost empty, with only a few

late-afternoon stragglers looking for an alcohol fix before the dinner crowd drifted in. Billy sat at the far end of the bar, watching the door.

As he entered, Jack felt gnawing hunger and realized he hadn't eaten since dawn. Between the river and the morgue, he'd lost his appetite and had been running on adrenaline. He signaled the barmaid and ordered a steak before Billy motioned him over to one of the empty booths.

Billy came over with two beers in his fist, slid in opposite Jack, and nudged across one of the bottles. They clanged glass, and each took a swig.

"So what do you have?" Jack asked eagerly.

"Slow down, *kemosabe*," Billy said, taking his sweet time lighting up a cigarette. "You first."

Jack recounted the basic facts of the case, keeping the details close to his vest. He knew Billy was dying to spill. His steak arrived, and he sliced into it as Billy began his tale.

"It's a paper deal," Billy offered. "Your dead man bought the papers off a college student who had dropped out and returned to the village."

Jack nodded his *okay*, tucking into the savory plate. *Keep coming*, he motioned with the steak knife.

"Jun Wah Chang is really Yao Sing Chang, one of the village orphans."

Jack took a gulp of beer, trying to digest the new information. He wouldn't be surprised if the Gees were running a paper operation like many of the other associations were doing—getting their members to America by any means necessary.

"He called, looking for work in Chinatown restaurants. They thought he was calling from Canada."

"Wait." Jack emphasized with the point of the serrated knife. "You're getting all this from the guy at Gee's who didn't know nothing from nothing this morning? But somehow from then to now, he suddenly remembers the guy's whole life in China?" He could almost see Billy blushing red in the dim blue light.

"Maybe he called the village, all right?"

"Why so helpful all of a sudden?"

"Maybe because I conned him into thinking it was better to have you as a friend than as an enemy."

"He didn't seem to care this morning," Jack said.

"Maybe he realized you can fix some traffic tickets or something."

"Funny. *Ha-ha*."

"Hey, he volunteered it," Billy mock groused. "What the fuck do I care? You want the rest of it or what?"

"Shoot."

"Since Yao's an orphan," Billy continued, "the Gee Association will pay for the cremation and services, whatever, on behalf of the village."

"When?"

"The wake is tomorrow morning at Wah Fook."

"So fast?"

"It's symbolic, yo. You think anybody's checking the ashes? They can bury him anytime. Whenever the cremation's done. It's all potter's field anyways."

"What time?"

"Nine to noon. They already posted an obit in the Chinese papers."

"Ceremonial," Jack observed. "What cemetery?"

"You gotta check with Wah Fook." Billy seemed amused,

watching Jack carve off pieces of Kim's legendary rib eye, devouring them.

"Any other surprises?" Jack asked as they clanged the last of their beers. Billy chortled like a villain.

"You know those phone numbers on the menu paper?" Billy paused for effect as Jack waited for the punch line. "They're restaurants all owned by Bossy Gee."

BOSSY GEE LIT up a few lights in Jack's head. *Prominent Chinatown businessman, big shot with the Hip Ching Association. Owns a bunch of Chinatown buildings.* His family had a long local history, with connections to Hong Kong and Taiwan.

"The eight-eight-eight prefix on those restaurant numbers?" Billy offered. "Bossy's idea. The Lucky Eights. *Bot bot bot.* The Triple Eights."

Gamblers' numbers, suckers' payout. He wondered if it was all just coincidence. Bossy Gee had been investigated by the Organized Crime Control Bureau (OCCB) for alleged ties to local *tongs.* Bossy Gee was known as the black sheep of the Gees. Not surprising that the association wouldn't want to get dragged into any of his endeavors.

"The Lucky Dragon and Lucky Phoenix he acquired in a fire sale. The previous Fukienese owner's daughter got shot and killed outside the Lucky Dragon. And the Lucky Phoenix was in debt after their accountant cooked the books and disappeared. Now Bossy's leasing out the two joints to new Fuks."

That explained the bleak and beat-down feel of the Lucky restaurants. They hadn't been so lucky for the operators, first-generation Chinese immigrants in the South Bronx, more grist for the grind of ghetto crime.

Billy ordered another round of beers, snuffed out his cigarette butt. "The other two, China Village and Golden City," Billy continued, "Bossy's had them a long time. Guess they're doing okay."

Jack remembered the modified Chinatown-restaurant business models he'd visited. He finished his steak, recalling, *Bossy Gee had two sons, one who joined the Marines, and another who joined the Black Dragons. One boy had a soldier's dream; the other has a criminal record.*

The beers arrived, and Jack decided to pace himself, figuring he'd have a long night ahead. Now he had even more questions than answers, and questions in Chinatown rarely led in just one direction. He knew it was too late to find Ah Por and decided to visit her in the morning with the knockoff wristwatch.

Someone started up the jukebox with Gloria Estefan's "Cuts Both Ways." It reminded him of Alexandra, but the warm and soft images of Alex naked in bed were crowded out by the memory of the cold and hard body on the refrigerated rack at the morgue.

He resisted the urge to call her.

"You hang out here," Billy instructed. "I gotta close up the tofu shop. Then I'll take the old Mustang outta Confucius, and we'll go for a ride."

"Where?" Jack asked skeptically.

"Didn't you say Yao had gambling problems in the Bronx? You mentioned Fay Lo's, right?"

"You know where Fay Lo's is?"

"No, but I know how to get there."

Jack shot him a *you-must-be-high* look.

"There's a car, or minivan, that goes there," Billy added.

"To Fay Lo's?" Jack pressed.

"It's like a junket, I hear. For the seniors, the old fart playas." Billy grinned. "We can follow them."

"Who?" Jack quizzed. "Where?"

"The minivan waits on Doyers. I think it's a Ghost racket. Takes the old-timers to the tracks and titty bars, to Chinese gambling Bronx-style." The Ghost Legion connection made Jack think about his onetime blood brother, Lucky Louie, Ghost *dailo* boss, who was useless to him now, lying in a coma at Downtown Medical.

"When?" asked Jack.

"I'll be back in an hour," Billy said as he left the booth.

The door slammed behind him, and the song on the jukebox ended. Grampa's was quiet again as Jack tried to find some connection between Chinatown and the Chinese in the Bronx, tried to work his way back through the clues and the questions doing a lion dance in his head.

He'd heard all the usual hard-luck tales from waiters and kitchen help, Chinese workingmen who'd been seduced by the idea of *luck*—every poor man's chance to be emperor— recklessly wagering two weeks', even a *month's* pay on the nose of a horse or a dog, the flip of a card or the turn of a number.

The truth was they were desperate for luck, anguished over believing that they could change the miserable, hope-less cast of their low workingmen's existence. They were gambling with their lives.

Finishing his beer, Jack pulled out his cell phone and called Alexandra. Her cheery greeting went to voice mail, and he hung up. He didn't like not getting an answer, and he hated to leave personal messages. Instead he dropped some coins into the jukebox and waited for the song that had briefly brought him back to tender moments with Alex.

Muscle Mustang

BILLY POWERED THE old Mustang out of the underground garage at Confucius Towers. It was only a few blocks to Grampa's, but he made a right on Bowery, gassed up on Houston Street, and took a quick cruise through the mean streets of the Lower East Side. Another right, going east, and the streets were wet and black. He rolled through the extended settlements of Chiu Chaos, Malaysians, and Vietnamese, continuing east to Essex, crossing Delancey into areas once Jewish, then Puerto Rican, and now Fukienese *Fuk Jo* land.

He circled back toward Grampa's, past the housing projects on South Street, quietly amused as he thought about Jack, his Chinatown friend, the *jook sing* cop who was conflicted about whether he was more American or more Chinese.

But it was never that complicated for Billy; all he had to do was look in the mirror. And in New York City, it never took much for someone to call you *Chink* and remind you who you were.

He'd been more than happy to help Jack, even happier now that the trail was leading to gambling and drinking and titty bars. It'd been a long time since he'd visited the Bronx anyway.

He patted the compact Beretta nine-millimeter semiau-tomatic pistol under his jacket and checked the dashboard lights as Grampa's neon bar sign beckoned down East Broadway.

Rollin' Dirty

JACK STEPPED OUT of Grampa's as the black Mustang pulled up. He opened the passenger door, saving Billy a rise out of the driver's bucket seat. *Muscle car*, thought Jack, *tinted windows, mag wheels, chrome runner*. The car looked old, but the engine was growling like it'd been souped up. The worst kind of gang-boy getaway car you could drive through an anticrime sector and not expect to get stopped for drugs and weapons, especially in the South Bronx.

"Haven't seen this car in a while," Jack said, sliding into the passenger seat. "What happened to the Range Rover?"

"The ex-wife got the Rover, that bitch," Billy spat out. "But this bad boy gets me where I need to go."

"No doubt," Jack agreed.

They drove behind Confucius Towers and turned off Bowery onto Pell Street. Billy killed the headlights before he made the sharp left onto Doyers, going slowly up the inclining street, and pulled over when he saw the minivan around the bend.

Two old men wearing oversized down jackets and hunting caps approached the minivan. They were joined by three other old men. The driver fired up his lights, popped the door, and waved the men in.

The seniors looked like restaurant workers—waiters and *da jop* kitchen help—the kind you'd see inside the homey little Chinatown coffee shops or at the local OTB picking the ponies. They were the last stragglers from the old bachelor generation lost in America.

They reminded Jack of his pa, who had been buried for six months in the pastoral grounds of Evergreen Cemetery. The traditional Ching Ming grave-sweeping ceremonies would be observed by the Chinese in the coming weeks.

The minivan crossed Chatham Square, went down Catherine Street to catch the FDR on South Street. Billy followed it, a few car lengths back. When they hit the highway, Billy turned on the dash radio, and the rock station blared out an old Steppenwolf number. Billy cranked up the radio, slapping the steering wheel and bellowing along with his own misunderstood lyrics:

> *Roarin' down the highway,*
> *Cruising for adventure,*
> *To whatever breaks our way . . .*

Jack allowed Billy his two minutes of *wild man*, figuring the song was ending. When it segued to a commercial, Jack turned off the radio and asked, "They run a van up every night?"

"Not sure *every* night," Billy answered. "But definitely weekends."

"Their gambling jones so bad they need to go to the Bronx?"

"Yeah," Billy said, keeping the minivan in sight. "Chinese love to gamble. It gives the working stiffs an excuse to hang out, have a few drinks, maybe score some pussy."

A one-night escape from the shackles of their lost China dreams.

The lights across the East River danced, neon colors shimmering off the dark waters, the city lights of Brooklyn and Queens sparkling in the distance like a scattering of jewels. A full moon was frozen overhead.

Cruising at sixty miles an hour, the Mustang rolled low to the blacktop, its mag wheels biting into the curves of the undulating highway. The outer boroughs flashed by on the other side of the river as the black car muscled its way north toward the Willis Avenue Bridge.

Billy said, "You know what? You mentioned the Harlem River, right? My first thought, the niggas killed him. Or the spics. You know? The usual, ripping off the takeout boys. You know the deal. Chinese always getting fucked in the South Bronx, yo."

Jack didn't offer a comment to that but knew he'd likely have to check in with the South Bronx precincts to see what the crime profile was against Asian Americans and also to get the lay of the land. *Rob the guy, sure, but dump him in the river? What kind of gangbanger would go through that much trouble to rob a deliveryman?*

"Those motherfuckers," Billy continued. "But I ain't worried. I got my shit." He patted the steel next to his ribs. "Punks don't scare me."

"You packing?" Jack asked, alarmed.

"Shit *yeah.*" Billy proudly flashed the gun inside his jacket. "Nine millimeter. *Beretta.* No boolshit."

"Fuck, Billy. You should have told me that *before* I got in the car."

"What the *fuck?*"

"You forget I'm a cop?"

"You think I'm rollin' dirty?" Billy spat back. "I'm *licensed*, brother. Permit to carry. Straight up. Would I compromise your ass? I'm hurt. I got a businessman's license because I carry and transfer *phat* stacks of dollars to the bank. A lot of Chinatown merchants got carry permits." He blew out a breath and kept the Mustang behind the minivan. "Wow . . . so all right?" he said with a smirk. "We cool?"

Jack took a breath and nodded *okay,* but he'd have to watch out for Billy's bad temper and his drinking. Not let him drive if he got anywhere near drunk. In the South Bronx, of all places.

Jack rolled down the window and let the freezing wind buffet his face as they approached the Willis Avenue Bridge.

"You still packing that thirty-eight?" Billy asked.

"Yeah."

"You still carrying that *shorty*? For *real*? You kidding me. Every nigga with a nine out there, and you with that peashooter thirty-eight?"

The minivan bounced in the distance.

"Shit, Jacky, fourteen nines in a clip, against six thirty-eights? Damn, you *must* be high, whatever you're thinking."

Jack had considered it, after the near-fatal encounter in Seattle. In his mind's eye he saw it again, his six-shot speedloader slipping into the Colt's open cylinder at the approach of a *tong* enforcer with a semiautomatic in his fist, aiming for the kill shot. It was a nightmare he'd have to tell the NYPD shrink about.

The thought made him think about Alexandra, how she'd saved his life, but with the Bronx waiting in the distance, he kept his eyes on the minivan. He'd considered switching over to a Smith & Wesson semiautomatic, a nine-millimeter piece, but most cops were favoring the new Glocks. The Glock 19 was a light twenty-three ounces unloaded, with a polymer frame and a fifteen-shot magazine. Hard to fault. But not a conversation he wanted with Billy.

Jack also knew that, like Billy, other cops favored the Berettas. Italian made, and also a NATO standard. Then there was Smith & Wesson, flying the American flag. The M69 series was a double action, twenty-six ounces unloaded with a stainless alloy frame. It held thirteen shots and featured a combat trigger.

Bottom line, Jack figured, *fifteen shots are better than thirteen*. Those last two shots could save your life, which he knew was what most NYPD cops believed. The Glock was lightweight and had the top capacity with the least recoil.

He'd have to make a change soon.

They crossed the bridge, and Jack quickly scanned the dark river below, wondering again where Chang's body had entered the water.

The Mustang blazed past Mott Haven and Hunts Point toward Pelham Bay. Before they knew it they'd crossed over into Westchester, the highway signs and the minivan leading them to the city of Yonkers and the racetrack.

What Jack remembered about Yonkers was that it was home to a large Irish and Italian population, and that the city had refused to desegregate its public-school system. In many ways, it was cop land.

A big billboard beckoned them to Yonkers Raceway.

* * *

Trotters

AT YONKERS RACEWAY the horses didn't gallop around a mile-long track with diminutive jockeys on their backs, Jack knew, like at Aqueduct or Belmont Park. Instead, *drivers* sat in sulky rigs pulled by horses that trotted unnaturally around a half-mile oval.

The old men went to the half-empty spectator grandstand and stood by the railing, the only Chinese at the track. Billy parked the car, and they walked to a spot near the men. Jack watched as Billy sidled up to them, eavesdropping at first, then engaging in small talk. Afterward, he drifted away toward the teller windows to place his bets.

The men stayed put, and Jack realized that they'd already made their bets with the Chinatown bookies involved with the junket operation.

Billy came back with a program and a fistful of tickets, surprising Jack by giving him three of them.

"I overheard their bets," Billy bragged. "Maybe we'll get lucky."

The horses on Jack's tickets, according to the program, were named Emperor's Sword, Dragon's Tale, and, to Jack's amazement, Alexandra's Choice. Their race position numbers spanning the first three races were 3, 6, and 8, all lucky Chinese numbers. The number 3 was a magic number. The number 6 sounded like "luck" in Cantonese, and number 8, *bot*, implied riches.

Jack wasn't surprised that the men had bet on those numbers, and probably *not* on the names of the horses.

A moving gate led the sulkies to the start, and suddenly they were off, the horses trotting furiously for position. The

spectators all watched the colorful numbers on the eight
sulkies chasing the leader around the oval track.

Lucky

THEY WON TWO out of the three races, placing in the
third, with Billy whooping it up alongside the old men. He'd
gotten close and had established a gambler's *hingdaai*, or
"camaraderie."

Jack figured it could come in handy later. His three
tickets won him sixty-six dollars, which he offered back to
Billy, who wouldn't hear of it.

The three races had taken almost an hour. For the time
being, they were all winners.

"Let's go," Billy said as the men headed back toward the
minivan. "They're going to the strip joint next."

That'll be another hour, thought Jack, *but we can wait in the car.*

They followed the minivan onto the highway and back to
the Bronx. Traffic was light going south, and Billy had to slow
down so as not to get too close to the minivan. He tapped
the radio and another Steppenwolf tune rocked out.
Pounding the steering wheel, he again mangled the lyrics.

> . . . *On a magic carpet ride!*
> *Spread your thighs girl,*
> *Open wide girl,*
> *Let your fantasy take you away!*

Jack wondered if Billy had managed to sneak a drink at
the track.

"Perfect!" Billy declared as the song ended. "They said there was a Korean stripper in from Seoul. A real knockout. Goes by the name Soomi."

"Good for *them*. We'll wait in the car," Jack said, still worried about Billy's drinking.

"You kiddin' me?"

"C'mon Billy, that's all just titillation."

"Well, you got the *tit* part right," Billy said sardonically.

"It's crass, Billy," Jack said.

"It's *ass*, brother. Trust me, I won't get you in trouble. You promised that lawyer lady you'd be a good boy or something?"

Jack smiled but didn't dignify Billy's poke at Alexandra with an answer.

"Okay," he relented. "But just one beer."

"One's all we need, bro." Billy grinned. "And it ain't the beer I'm thinking about."

The entire trip took about twenty-five minutes. They parked under the overpass as the minivan stopped down the block from a big flashing sign that announced BOOTY. Silhouettes of naked dancers flanked a smaller sign with the words GENTLEMEN'S CLUB.

"Yeah Booty's!" Billy cheered.

"You been here before?" Jack asked.

"Just once. One of my customers threw a Christmas party here."

A huge black bouncer guarded the door, a bald, six-foot-five, three-hundred-pound load of hurt. He could have been a lineman for one of the local football teams. "Booty" rang a bell in Jack's head as he tried to recall something from old police blotters, something about Bronx mafiosi and Latin Lords drug dealers teaming up to take over the area's vice rackets. Jack imagined that, like most jiggle joints, Booty's was mobbed up.

A few blocks away, he could hear the rumble of a Metro North train, and in the far distance the lights of the George Washington Bridge twinkled. Farther south, he could make out the façade of Yankee Stadium. In the darkness, he realized they were near the Highbridge section where he'd been earlier in the morning.

"The homies nicknamed this place *Chino*'s," Billy said, "because of all the Chinese waiters and market guys from Hunts Point who used to come here."

They watched the old men enter the club and, against Jack's better instincts, followed them. The black bouncer barely noticed them, just another bunch of little *Chinamen*.

T. A. P. *tits. ass. pussy.*

BOOTY'S WAS DEEP and wide. In a past life it might have been a garage or an auto repair shop. Now one of the long walls had been mirrored, in front of which a narrow runway, like a catwalk, supported the prancing of the dancers. There was a pole at either end. Under the dramatic play of track lights above, the scene was like a raunchy off-Broadway musical. *Way way off-Broadway*, thought Jack.

Along the opposite wall was a long bar where you could get a tiny slice of pizza with your second overpriced drink. Some twenty little tables in two long lines filled the rest of the space.

There weren't that many Chinese from what Jack could

see in the otherwise dim lighting. There were a few other Asians—he couldn't tell what kind, Filipino or Cuban maybe—but most of the patrons on this cold night were black and Latino, many wearing Yankees or Knicks caps and sweatshirts.

Jack waited by the bar across from where the runway began and ordered a beer just to hold his spot there.

Billy made his way to the area where the old men sat, at the other end of the runway. He ingratiated himself by buying them a round of the joint's watered-down beer with the cash they'd helped him win. He ordered a Jack Daniel's for himself, also probably watered down.

"Gangsta's Paradise" played over the loudspeakers, and the girls on the runway—two white, one black—continued dancing. They wore dangerously high heels, G-strings, and barely there bikini tops. They stole glances at themselves in the wall mirror that was angled to reflect full-body views as they swayed and gyrated under the stage lights. They knew their poses well, letting their breasts dangle just right, *perfect*, with their lower parts beckoning whenever they bent over.

The men nearest to the runway got their dollar bills ready. *More, gimme more. Yeah, right there, baby girl, culo, clika.*

Flesh trade, Jack thought, *they got that terminology right.*

The girls worked through their simulated pornographic poses. One of the white girls humped the end pole while sucking on a long red blow job lollipop.

"*Hom lun*," one of the old men chortled in Cantonese. *Suck cock.*

The second girl, a bootylicious black princess, played with a pink dildo as she spread her legs open to a bow-and-arrow pose, pretending to jam herself.

"*Eww hei*," another of the old men said in Toishanese. *Fucking pussy*.

The other white dancer, near the first pole, went from a pile-driver pose, which exposed her bottom, to crawling on all fours, which brought a chorus of *wooo*s from the crowd.

The music pounded on.

The men seated farther back folded their dollar bills into little airplanes and hurled them like darts toward the stage. As if on cue, the three dancers pulled aside their G-strings, momentarily revealing shaved and waxed labia and anuses to the delight of the men. The music amped up even more, and a crew of pink-wigged waitresses made their rounds.

The old men nursed their beers and waited for the Korean girl.

The dancers gathered up their dollar bills and changed places on the runway to give the other customers an equal-opportunity viewing. And to suck up more money. After another ten minutes, the song changed to "Waterfalls," and the dancers gleefully squirted each other's privates with water pistols shaped like phalluses. There was another set of lewd poses—standing doggie, reverse cowgirl, missionary spread—as the girls on the ends spun around, rubbing their crotches and butts against the long, hard poles, wearing only their G-strings now.

Jack figured they'd been there almost half an hour.

A new rotation began as an Asian girl stepped to the front end of the runway and started her routine at the first pole, farthest from Billy and the old men. Jack could see they were eager for her to dance her way to their section.

The pop/rap beats changed to a rendition of "Sukiyaki." Jack frowned at the racial overtones playing out but couldn't take his eyes off her. The Korean girl named Soomi sexy-strolled around the pole amid a chorus of low moans from the men nearest her. Soomi was a knockout, drop-dead sexy gorgeous, a perfect voluptuous body on a Victoria's Secret frame, almost six feet tall, strutting atop sequined *fuck-me* high heels. She wore a tiny glittering G-string and a transparent brassiere that showcased her large budding nipples.

Someone yelled "Kimchi!" and she giggled.

She had a pretty Asian face framed by long black hair, an exotic-fantasy look that captivated the mostly non-Asian audience of lechers and perverts. Jack didn't count himself among them but couldn't help admiring her beauty, and even though he'd expected it to be this way in places like this, he was still turned off by the bestial behavior of the men in this so-called *gentlemen*'s club.

Soomi continued her routine by bending over and adjusting her platform heels. There were more hoots as Billy came over to Jack, licking his lips at the closer view.

"She got a butt like Jennifer Lopez," he crooned. "Lips like a blowhole, titties bouncing like Jell-O!"

Jack shook his head, took a pull from his bottle of warming beer. Billy was mesmerized, hypnotized, like all the men, gunned down by Soomi's raw, visceral display of her shaved womanhood. *Like a prime cut of sashimi*, considered Billy, *more yellowtail hamachi than red toro. Brown eye, in the other men's eyes.* She offered a sweet smile to the men seated near the runway who were laying money at her feet. She paraded in front of them, kicking the bills toward the mirror wall, removing her see-through bra in teasing stages.

"Sukiyaki" remixing over the speakers.

A few gyrations, shaking her JLo booty, and she had her bra off, tossing it mischievously at the mirror. *Million-dollar breasts with puffy nipples.* She saw in the glass how beautiful she really was. *A blessing.* A squadron of dollar airplanes crashed into the mirror wall near her. She spread her feet apart, bent over, waved to the crowd between her legs, her long black hair pooling onto the stage. Then she slowly straightened up, turned, and braced her back against the glass wall. She spread her feet wide again, cupped her breasts in her hands, and stroked her nipples with her thumbs until they were hard and stubby.

Crumpled balls of paper money plopped and bounced onto her end of the runway. Soomi pulled up the shiny front patch of her G-string, and more dollar bills appeared at her feet. She wiggled the string so that it nestled into the folds of her fleshy labia. This provoked another round of moans from the front row. Billy winked at Jack, folded a few dollar airplanes, and went toward the front section.

Jack could see him pitching them in Soomi's direction as she slid to the floor and did a slow doggie crawl, slapping the assorted scatter of dollars toward the mirror. Billy wadded up a few more dollars and tossed them, like hand grenades, toward the other dancers. *Just like Billy*, mused Jack, *trying to keep everybody happy.*

Soomi smoothly shifted into a bow-and-arrow pose, spreading her legs into a horizontal V. With her free hand she pulled back on the G-string again so that it spread open her glistening lips. After a few moments, she rolled over and turned to the men on the other side. Come-hither smile on her face. She pulled the string back and forth again. *Everybody gets a peek.* Horny men with gaping mouths and astonished faces.

More. Gimme more.

The money rained down on her. She smiled, scanned the crowd, gave them a cute wave of her hand. Glancing at the old men, Jack saw them looking lustfully, longingly, in her direction. Jack knew that with their old eyes, and seated at the far end in the dim light, they were only getting a general impression of Soomi, not yet the intimate view they were hoping for. They patiently waited for her to make her way to them.

Soomi did a spread V, her womanhood facing the other way now. When she turned her rear toward Jack, looking back at him over her shoulder, he locked eyes with her. In that odd, frozen moment, he felt he saw a sister, and she a brother or an ex-boyfriend she'd left behind.

Soomi never looked his way again. She did another five minutes of standing doggie and reverse cowgirl with the long lollipop in her mouth. When the music signaled the new rotation, she skipped the end pole. Instead, she went back along the mirror wall, gathering up her dollar bills, stuffing them into what was probably a knockoff Prada bag. She quickly disappeared with her booty bag into a restricted dressing room that the club provided for the dancers.

Jack could see the disappointment on the old faces. They'd waited forty-five minutes and had only gotten a cheap, distant glimpse. Maybe the sight of all the jiggling flesh made them feel like young men again, Jack thought, but at the rate of twenty bucks just for a lap dance, none of them were, in Billy's words, going to *score some pussy* here tonight. Billy might be able to afford the imported ladies at Angelina Chao's, but these old men would probably wait until the junket brought them back to Chinatown and the cheap whores, *yau leng yau peng*, at Fat Lily's. *Temporarily young again for one-third the price.*

"Bitch is dissing her own people," Billy groused into Jack's ear.

"She's Korean," Jack answered. "Not Chinese."

"You know what I mean," Billy bitched. "*Asian*. She too good for them?"

Jack, even as cynical as he'd become, didn't see it that way. Behind the sexy smile, what he'd seen in her eyes was sadness and shame.

They were just lonely old men, Jack figured, seeking their young memories in the wrong place.

"She looks like an angel," Billy continued. "But she's an evil gold-diggin' bitch. C'mon, *fuck* this."

Jack could see the old men were already getting up from their end tables, heading in the direction of the toilets.

"Let's go," Billy said. "We got better places to spend our fuckin' money."

They went out past the big bald bouncer and headed back to the car at the underpass. Looking back, Jack saw the bright signage that continued to shine out BOOTY.

Fat Man's Place

THE MINIVAN LED them south past Yankee Stadium to somewhere off the Grand Concourse, to a seemingly deserted street. Fay Lo's was the Fat Man's place, and Billy wanted to stay close enough to hook up with the group as they entered. He pulled up just past the corner as the minivan parked down the block from what looked like a closed diner-type restaurant. The sign above the graffitied roll-down gate advertised CHINA Y LATINA COMIDAS.

Jack imagined a Chinese Cuban, chino-Latino connection. Of the Chinese, the Chinese Cubans were here first, in the Bronx. Jack was sure there were fewer *chino–puerto ricanos*, *chino dominicanos*, *chino mexicanos* than there were Chinese Cubans.

It had taken them the better part of three hours, a circuitous trip through two boroughs and the county of Westchester, to finally arrive at Fay Lo's. It was close to midnight, the black sky now deeper than Chinese *mok* ink.

They caught up to the men as they entered a dimly lit alley next to the diner. The driver pressed a doorbell and looked up at a little camera recessed into the brick wall. There was a buzzer sound, and the driver pulled open the door, waving the men in past a big Chinese door goon. He stopped Billy, who pleaded, "We're all together!" A Toishanese chorus of "He's with us!" from the old men confirmed it, and the big goon let them through.

Against better judgment again, Jack entered, relaxing his grip on the badge in his pocket and the Colt holstered on his hip. They followed the group into a big room, softly lit so that it looked vaguely like the Asian gambling sections at the Atlantic City or Indian casinos. Featured were mostly Asian games—thirteen-card poker, mini-baccarat, Hong Kong–style stud—with small rooms in the back section for high-stakes mah-jongg, *fan tan* button bets, and *pai gow* dominoes. Also in the spread were a few standard casino games like blackjack, roulette, and a bank of slot machines just to keep the gamblers' girlfriends happy.

A pair of cute girls with cigarette trays casually offered

packs of Marlboros and Newports along with little shot bottles of Johnnie Walker Black and XO.

In the far corner they'd set up a buffet table of yellow rice and beans, some *pernil*, chicken stew, and Chinese *char siew*, roast pork.

The betting action was moderate, mostly Chinese men chain-smoking around the tables. They looked like the workers he'd seen in the Golden City and China Village and in Chinatown, throwing down their tip money, their hustle pay of sweaty dollar bills, looking for the long odds—twenty, thirty, a hundred to one.

The gang boys stood out from the civilian players. They wore black leather jackets, muscle tees, cargo pants. They propped up their colorful punk haircuts with gel and tagged Chinese "ghost" tattoos on the sides of their necks, fists, and biceps. Inky word characters needled into their skin. Proud of it. Swagger. Willing to fight and die for the gang family. Though it all aided law enforcement in identifying members by their gang tats and nicknames.

They looked just like all the other Chinatown gang-bangers Jack had grown up around. Some of them were posted near the corners of the big room while others patrolled along the periphery, keeping their distance from the main floor so as not to make the gamblers nervous.

Besides the cigarette girls, the only other two women in the place were "dragon ladies," fortyish *dai ga jeer* women who stayed back by the mah-jongg area and supervised the cigarette girls. They knew that Chinese men, when it came to gambling, regarded women as bad luck and wouldn't gamble next to them. *Luck don't be a lady tonight.* They also kept their distance from the main-floor action.

Jack spotted three cameras, managers watching every-body from a security room somewhere. The entire place could be closed off by electric roll gates that curled up inside the ceiling. They could lock down, in case of a raid, at the push of a button.

Not exactly a Chinatown mom-and-pop operation.

Jack wondered if the weekly take was as good as that of the Chinatown basements, which he knew was six figures of dirty *tong* money. It was early yet for the true night crawlers, but the loose action—maybe thirty or so players—followed in a flow that went to a wide stairway in the back. The steps led down into a basement area that was sectioned off for different bet-ting venues and entertainment. There were areas with big-screen TV coverage of satellite-beamed horse races from Hong Kong and China, but also from as regional as Golden Gate or Delta Downs. A complete OTB schedule. Another section with booths where you could play video poker or blackjack. There were a couple of older men in team jerseys, who Jack guessed were Chinese Cubans or Chinese South Americans by their darker complexions, taking sports bets next to cable-TV monitors. They posted hourly specials where they took bets on the house version of lotto, offered odds on different-colored fighting fish that tore each other to bloody shreds inside a glass aquarium. Gamblers could play number combinations at *sic bo*, high-low, or bet on colors and numbers on a long-odds Wheel of Fortune.

Something for everybody.

Only a dozen gamblers roamed around the basement, watched over by a pair of bored Ghosts.

Jack followed Billy back upstairs to the main floor. In the back of his mind he felt like they were being watched.

"Split up," Billy said. He went off toward the poker tables.

Jack avoided the Chinese poker games, which actually required focus and concentration, and instead went to the deserted *fan tan* table, which was situated near the middle of the floor. All he had to do there was bet on the number of buttons left over from a pile that a croupier separated into groups of four. He could watch the entire room from that vantage point.

He took out his winnings from Yonkers and started dropping casual bets onto the *fan tan* table. The croupier parsed out the ceramic buttons, slowly arriving at the remaining pieces, which would always number between one and four. *Simple.*

In the big card games area, he could see Billy betting along with the old men on *sup som jeung*—thirteen-card Chinese poker—and mini-baccarat. Billy accepted a shot glass of Johnnie Walker from one of the cigarette girls and threw it back in a single gulp. If they were being watched, betting separately in different areas would split the attention, and maybe they could fool them into thinking that they were really just two more gamblers out for a lucky roll. But now he knew he'd have to watch Billy's drinking. They were both armed, in an environment where the Ghosts were armed as well.

No trouble, Billy, Jack whispered to himself, almost like a prayer.

Billy continued spreading his Yonkers money across the poker tables. There were occasional bursts of laughter from the group there.

The *fan tan* croupier swept away his dollars, and Jack bet the box again, feigning attention this time. He could see how "Singarette" Chang, like other workingmen with dreams, could be sucked into the fake glamour of the gambling life. With a little luck, you could build up a bundle, but if you were unlucky, if the cards were flipped against you, then you could wind up with a ton of debt and heartache. Then the gang boys and the loan sharks would circle you in a frenzy.

He lost three straight *fan tan* games and took his remaining money to the roulette table. He bet the action groups and the colors, letting the wheel spin under the bouncing white ball while he continued to scan the room. While he was winning on red, a whoop and holler jumped out of Billy, which caught the Ghosts' attention.

Jack watched them size Billy up. *No trouble, Billy,* echoed in his mind. Scooping up his winnings, he moved next to Billy, hoping the Ghosts would let it pass. Giving him the eye-fuck nod, Jack said, "Let's roll. You got people peeping you now. I got the scene already, and there's nothing left but trouble." *It's not like I got a warrant or anything, but I got a peep of the guy's life in the months before he got himself killed.*

"And I still got a funeral in the morning," he spat out, steely when Billy hesitated, scanning the room.

"Okay, *chill,*" Billy acknowledged, spotting the Ghosts. "But I was on a winning streak."

"Me too," Jack lamented. "Me too."

"We the two sorriest winners ever had to leave a place because motherfuckers paying too much attention to us."

They exited Fay Lo's back alley with the baleful glare of the door goon following them.

They doubled back to the corner where Billy had parked the car.

Stinkin' Badges

JACK SAW IT in the flash of surprise and fear that crossed Billy's face. Turning, he reached for his Colt as two men appeared from the shadows near the Mustang. One black guy, one white, wearing ghetto street gear and approaching with swagger in a way that he couldn't see their hands.

Guns cleared holsters simultaneously as Jack and the men barked in unison.

"POLICE!"

"DROP YOUR WEAPON!"

The yelling froze them all with guns pointed in a standoff, hard faces not backing down but recognizing the same cop language.

Billy leaned away from Jack and kept his Beretta trained on the black man.

"Lower your weapon!" the white one demanded.

"*You* lower your weapon!" Jack responded. He sensed nervous fingers on triggers.

"Whoa, hold up!" the black one eased. "We're cops!"

"I know *I* am," Jack challenged. "Where's your shield?"

"Where's *yours?*" the white one shot back.

There was a moment's silence until Jack said, "Okay, easy does it. Show you *mine*. You show me *yours*." He slowly flapped open his jacket with his free hand, letting his gold badge glint in the night light.

The black man unzipped his Raiders sweatshirt so Jack could see the silver badge dangling off a beaded chain.

"What precinct?" Jack asked tensely.

"The Four-One, Bronx," the white man answered, pulling open his jacket to expose his own shield. "You?"

"Manhattan South," Jack answered, like the designation had more weight than the Ninth or the Fifth Precincts.

The men lowered their guns cautiously, except Billy.

"Put it away," Jack growled. Billy reluctantly complied, and the cops holstered their weapons as well.

Everyone took a breath.

"Wait, your partner's badge?" the black cop said.

"He's a civilian," Jack explained. "But he's got a permit."

Billy smiled and shrugged, showed his New York City license.

"Civilian? You pulled a piece on us?" the black cop complained.

"I'm carrying *fat* cash, bro. What the fuck? You think I'm just gonna give it up to someone looks like you, in a hoodie, moving at me? You got the wrong Chinaman, nigga." Billy had said *nigga* in a tone between street-brother acknowledgment and racist dagger.

The black cop shot Billy a *fuck-you* look, not liking being addressed that way by a Chink.

"Wait in the car," Jack told Billy, who stood defiantly for a moment. The way Jack repeated it to him made him back off and get into the Mustang.

"Why'd you pick *us*?" Jack asked the black cop pointedly.

"Wasn't you, or your *homie*," came the answer. "It was the car."

Billy's hoodmobile.

"Tinted windows, chrome wheels," the white cop added. "All the bad boys roll that way."

"You didn't expect two Chinese though?" Jack asked.

"*Whatever*. It's the South Bronx. Anything rolls, anything goes."

"What're y'all doing around here?" the black cop asked Jack.

"I'm working a homicide. We pulled a body out of the river."

"Wait a minute," the white cop said. "Was that the one came over the radio this morning?"

"Right," Jack answered.

"Two of our uniforms were on the Harbor boat. First on the scene," the white cop added. "They said it looked like a jumper."

Jack didn't comment, said, "I caught a lead. Anyway, you guys got any problems in this sector?"

"Sure, lotsa problems here. Prostitution. Drugs. All the fuckin' drunks after Yankee games. Whaddya looking for?"

"Anything around these adjacent blocks?" Jack scanned the empty streets.

"Why? You got something happened around here?"

"Not sure," Jack hedged. "Anything related to robberies, gang activity, or violent crimes?"

"Just punk asses from the projects," the black cop said, "snatching handbags and chains from the subway. Or beating up white students from the Catholic schools."

The white cop thought for a moment. "You mean *Asian*-related incidents, don't you?"

"Right," Jack said. "Anything?"

"We don't keep records that way."

"Yeah, but you know what I mean," Jack pushed.

The two undercover cops exchanged glances before the black one answered.

"Matter of fact, a coupla months ago," he said, smirking, "there was a fight or something just around the block. A truck driver called it in. A Chinese kid got beat up pretty bad. We found him laying in the street. But he claimed he didn't know who assaulted him, couldn't press charges."

Going to settle it himself? wondered Jack.

"There were a few Chinese on the street," he continued, "but nobody witnessed anything."

"How was it called in?" Jack asked. "Did the truck driver describe the fighters?"

The white cop hesitated before answering. "He said a bunch of Chinks were kung fu fighting."

They all turned as Billy fired up the Mustang, keeping the lights off.

Jack's face twisted from a sad smile to a frown as he asked, "What else?"

"Some of the kid's friends came by, said they'd take him to Bronx Medical."

"You get a name?" Jack asked.

"He said some bogus name, Dew Lay or something."

Dew lay meant "fuck you" in Cantonese, the assault victim blowing off the white *gwai lo* cop.

"That's it?" Jack said.

"Right. No charges, no case."

Yeah, just some crazy Chinks kung fu fightin' on a Saturday night in the Four-One, thought Jack, but he backed his gratitude with a handshake as the two undercovers moved off.

The adrenaline from the armed face-off was draining off now, and he slipped back into the Mustang, watching the plainclothes cops in their unmarked car roll off into the dark Bronx distance. *Lucky they were cops,* thought Jack, *it could have been a trigger-happy nightmare.* There had been a spate of shootings of black off-duty cops by white off-duty cops.

"Lucky for *them*," Billy said, firing the headlights and driving in the opposite direction. "I woulda iced them if they weren't cops."

Exactly, thought Jack. He'd had enough of Billy's help for one night.

"C'mon," Billy said, "enough is enough. I'll drive you home, bro. Unless you want to go for *siew yeh* snacks."

"Home sounds good," answered Jack.

"I bet." Billy nosed the black car back toward Brooklyn.

THE RIDE BACK was relatively quiet—no Steppenwolf, no rock 'n' roll—with just some generic news station that Billy had switched to. Neither man spoke, watching the highway and the night beyond.

Jack knew Billy was savoring the flavors of his night's exploits, and Billy knew Jack was preoccupied, turning over whatever clues he had in his mind. Cop work. He had a homicide, a body with two names, a set of keys, and an unknown motive. They passed that section of the Harlem River where Sing's body was discovered earlier in the morning. *Where the victim worked, where he gambled, maybe. Was it just over a gambling debt?* Billy worked his way through traffic. *But who collects from a dead man? It didn't make sense to kill him. Was it a robbery? But why go through the trouble to dump him in the river? How much of a debt costs someone his life? And how come no ID?*

Traffic thinned out, and Billy had them rolling through Sunset Park before the weight of the day's events could finally settle, take hold.

Money—Ah Por's words—the root of all evil.

Home

JACK SAT ON the edge of his bed and stripped, thinking he'd get a few hours' sleep before the visit to the Chinatown funeral parlor where Sing's pre-cremation wake would be held. He didn't know if it was the fatigue from the twenty-four-hour murder shift or the cheap beer at Booty's or the drinks at Grampa's and Fay Lo's that was dragging him down.

He closed his eyes, saw glimpses of Alex's naked curves, the lean angles of her arms and legs. He took another breath, imagining an herbal scent in her hair. *Hips, thighs, breasts*, firm and soft where he'd caressed them. Places that became hard upon his touch.

He remembered taking a deep cleansing breath, still remembering Alex's wet and tender places. Then his head hit the pillow, and he went down for the count.

Field of Dreams

THE COUNT DIDN'T go to oblivion, but to a series of disjointed dreams and images.

He saw himself, nighttime at the racetrack. He's in the grandstand watching a racing filly named Alexandra pulling a sulky around the oval track. She's hopelessly boxed in along the rail by the other horses and their rigs.

The dream jumped to:

Naked women cavorting to a remix of "Sukiyaki" in a strip club. Cascading money, with Billy throwing folded-dollar airplanes at the topless dancers.

Cops silently lingering over a dead body floating in the river.

The sequence jumped again to:

Gritty piles of money for bets on a pair of colorful fighting fish separated in a square tank at Fay Lo's gambling joint. An explosion in the water, bloody fins and organs flying as the frenzied fish tear each other to shreds.

Silence over Yao "Singarette's" corpse on the steel slab at the morgue, from possible suicide to homicide in a single thrust.

The root of all evil. Ah Por's words breaking the silence.

Following the dreams was a dizzying kaleidoscope of images. Freudian stuff he'd prepared for the NYPD shrink.

A pit bull lunging at him out of the ghetto project's darkness.

A Chinese *tong* enforcer bearing down on him as he frantically tries to reload.

His Colt revolver clicking on empty chambers.

Lucky, Chinatown ex–blood brother and Ghost Legion street-gang boss, suddenly sitting up out of his hospital coma.

The last image jolted Jack awake in his bed. He tried to get back to sleep but wound up drinking green tea and thinking about the Wah Fook funeral parlor as morning light crept into the bedroom.

For Jong

THE WAH FOOK still had the nineteenth century baroque façade from when it was the Bacigalupe Funeral Home, with the relief columns and sculptural decorations still visible on old buildings throughout Chinatown and Little Italy.

Jack remembered the Italian mob in Chinatown used to store its illegal Fourth of July fireworks that it hawked on Canal Street in the Bacigalupe basements.

Plastic signage in Chinese covered over the Bacigalupe name that had been carved into the stone above the portico entrance.

There were two old lanterns above the bronze entrance doors on which seven death notices—white tickets with the Chinese names of the dead—had been posted. Jack saw the one closest to what he was looking for, Jun Wah Zhang, and went inside. He badged the manager, who led him past the two wakes in progress to a smaller room at the end of the corridor and turned on the ceiling lights. There was a closed casket there, but the room hadn't been set up for a wake yet.

On a small table to one side, there was an urn. An inexpensive one you could find in any of the Chinatown curio shops. Dark glazed ceramic, featuring bronze mountains and green scenery of leaves and trees. Colors of the earth. Big enough to hold all the remains of what was once a man.

No picture.

Nothing but a Chinese name in black ink on a white scrap of paper. A name that wasn't even really his, a name he'd purchased.

"What can you tell me about him?" Jack asked.

"The association paid for the urn, the *for jong* cremation, and the burial in their field at the cemetery."

"It's empty now?" Jack asked, looking at the urn. *Fire interred.*

"Yes. When we receive the ashes we'll repack them in the urn. Then it goes out for burial with the next procession."

"That's it?"

"As far as we know." The manager shrugged.

The urn was set on the side in a dark room because Jun was an orphan, and though there'd be an obituary posted quickly in the *Sing Tow Journal*, no one really expected anyone to come.

The manager dimmed the lights and left Jack sitting on a solitary folding chair near the back wall.

Jack thought he'd visit Ah Por next for more clues, since he was only two blocks from the Seniors' Center. He figured he'd also check South Bronx hospitals for recent Asian victims of assault.

He was looking toward the closed casket, hoping it was empty, when he caught her out of the corner of his eye: a woman in a cherry-red down jacket coming into the room, stopping, and looking toward the urn. She hadn't noticed him in the dim light by the back wall.

She'd surprised him, not only because he didn't expect anyone to come—except maybe Billy's friend from the Gee Association—but because no Chinese ever wore red to a wake. *So it must have been a surprise to her, too.* She couldn't have expected to come here.

She looked to be in her late twenties, short hair, a rugged red windburn on her cheeks. A sad face now as she approached the urn table. From the bottom shelf of the table she grabbed a stack of paper, *death money*, lit it, and dropped it, flaming, into a blackened brass bucket. A bribe to the gods for mercy in the next world. She plucked three sticks of incense and lit them, bowed three times before the urn, and stuck the incense sticks into a cup there. She shook her head, whispered a few quiet words.

Before Jack could move, she rushed out.

She was already out the front door when Jack stepped from the room. He zipped up his jacket and went out to Mulberry Street after her.

He followed her north toward Canal Street, keeping a half-block behind so as not to spook her. Stepping quickly, she wore a black turtleneck sweater under the bright jacket that meant she was still celebrating the Chinese New Year.

Almost to Canal, he saw her slip into the driver's side of one of the Ford vans parked along the street, the vans carrying the cardboard crates of fruits for the day's sidewalk market.

Jack stopped, waited at a distance. The simple rub-on letters on the van's front doors identified them as Chong Vihn Produce, a warehouse address in Brooklyn. *Vietnamese Chinese*.

He considered the two new Vietnamese noodle joints on the street, knew the Viets all supported one another's businesses.

The curbside market vendors on the Mulberry-Canal corner were the only ones open for business in the bitter cold and slushy mess. They'd shoveled off the curb, stacked out the crates on folding tables, and took turns warming up in the vans.

Jack knew the sidewalk merchants supported the local restaurants in exchange for use of the toilet facilities whenever needed.

A street community, Jack knew.

Business was brisk considering the light traffic on the streets. He figured a couple of tour buses must have rolled in, visitors to the fabled neighborhoods of Lower Manhattan. He was about to move to where he could get another view when the young woman in the red jacket stepped out of the van and took over one of the fruit stands from an older woman, who then retreated into the van.

The stands offered melons, pineapples, strawberries and grapes, cherries—fruits from the global season kept fresh in the New York City cold.

She'd relieved the cherry stand, her red jacket the perfect pitch for the cherries she started to bag for grab-and-go customers. Chinatown people snapped them up as tasty treats for the extended families, and tourists grabbed them for quick snacks.

Jack took a deep breath and exhaled into his hands. He wondered what her connection was to the orphan Yao Sing Chang, deliveryman, who was soon to be a pile of ashes in a Chinese urn.

He went toward the stand thinking he'd start the conversation by buying a bag of cherries, that, if he got the chance, he'd bring to Alex's office.

"One bag, please," he said with a small smile, handing her the dollar bills and watching her face.

She barely noticed him as she bagged the cherries and took his money.

"I saw you at the Wah Fook," Jack said quietly, not sure if she'd understand his English. He was ready to say it in Chinese when she glanced at him, saying, "*Chaai loh ah?* You're a cop?" in Cantonese.

He was gauging her face, flashing her his badge as he answered, "Yes." *She'd made him right away, immigrants seeing with sharper eyes, especially if they might be illegal.*

"What happened to him?" she asked.

"That's what I'm trying to find out," Jack answered.

"Another day"—she sighed—"another struggle."

"What?" Jack asked, hearing, *Biggie Smalls? Rap?*

"He had a tough time here," she said. "But he saved me once."

"How did you know him?" asked Jack, trying to hold her eyes.

She continued to bag the loose cherries. A group of Scandinavian tourists appeared and bought up all her bags.

"I can't talk now," she said, her cheeks darkening as she started bagging cherries again.

"When's better?" Jack asked, handing her his NYPD detective's card.

"I usually break for lunch at two," she answered.

He scanned the street. It wasn't the Mulberry Street he remembered, dotted now with overseas enterprises, distributorships, wholesalers' storefronts, a few restaurants.

"Xe Lua," he suggested, *Vietnamese.* "On your break?"

She looked down the street at Xe Lua's banner, a familiar flag.

"Okay," she said as other customers rushed by.

He doubled back toward the Seniors' Center, wondering if she'd actually show up, feeling her eyes on his back.

Old and Wise

HE FOUND AH Por quickly this time, in the same location as before, by the big back window near the exit door to the courtyard. She was watching one of the TV monitors when he sat and touched her hand. It took a moment for her to recognize Jack, the young image of his father.

He nodded and smiled, gave her Singarette's fake Rolex. And a folded Lincoln.

She looked at the knockoff, ran a thumb over it.

"Canal Street," she said, handing it back.

Sure, Jack thought, *Canal for knockoffs.*

He handed her the Yonkers racing program.

"*Som lok bat,*" she counted, "three, six, eight."

The program was unmarked, but she'd picked their three winning numbers.

What does it mean? wondered Jack as Ah Por dismissed him and went back to the TV monitor. He thanked her and left the beehive of age and wisdom.

Eddie's

HE WENT BACK to Mott Street, to Eddie's, where he took one of the small tables in the back and made calls over the noise of the Chinese News radio station.

It wasn't until the third call, to Saint Barnabas Hospital, that he got a hit. The staff had admitted an emergency case by the name *Dewey Lai*, an assault victim, ten nights earlier. *Dew Lay* again, their little joke, *fuck you.*

Jack requested that the hospital fax the pictures of the admittee, which it was required to take, to the main number at the Fifth Precinct. After all, he was already in the precinct.

He called Alexandra, feeling the bag of cherries in his

pocket. But all he got was the answering machine and her cheery voice.

He shifted his thoughts back to the body in the river.

Engine

Jack waited for the woman in the red jacket at Xe Lua. The place had a bamboo feel and a fake little inside bridge you crossed over to get to the back, where Jack took one of the side tables.

He was hoping she'd spill something good and thought about ordering a *for che touh*, Vietnamese beef-broth rice noodles with sliced meat, one of his antidotes to the New York City winter.

He kept an eye on the front door, turning over the past hours in his head. In murder cases, cops usually worried about the first forty-eight hours because they feel the perpetrator will flee the area and the jurisdiction.

Because the identification was missing, and because of the way the body was dumped, Jack didn't feel the time constraint. The killer wasn't thinking about fleeing, he figured. The perp wasn't sweating over having left evidence, over getting caught. He was counting on living in plain sight, like he regularly did. He'd just *washed* away the matter, *sai jo keuih*. Very devious of him, always thinking, one step ahead. *Maybe the vic would sink and never surface. Or it'd take so long that they'd barely recognize him as human when he did rise up. Even if he did float up, they'd never know who he really was, invisible illegal immigrant.*

Jack wasn't surprised that the Ghosts protected Fay Lo's.

But the Chinese beatdown raid? Did it have anything to do with anything other than the usual gang beef? Chinatown's dominant gang had its fingers everywhere. But in the Bronx? Had the Chinese Cubans, the *chino cubanos*, built up alliances? *Who knows?* Was it all just about a gambling debt? The Ghosts were challenged by the Dragons everywhere they operated. Was someone trying to make an example of *Singarette*?

SHE WALKED IN, the red jacket glowing, exchanging greetings with the waitstaff, the cashier, obviously a regular here. She spotted Jack and demurely took a seat at his table, aware of the attention swinging her way. He half rose and poured her a cup of hot tea, addressing her politely.

"*Dim yeung ching foo nei?*" he asked. "How should I address you?"

"Just call me Huong," she answered, a slight Vietnamese accent on her Hong Kong Cantonese now. *Huong*, remembered Jack, meant "rose" in Vietnamese. *The color red again.* She had a robust aura about her, a wholesome look. *Mature fruit, but not old tofu.*

Wasting no time, she ordered a *bun cha gio*, vegetarian vermicelli, to his hearty pho engine, *for che touh*.

"It's freezing out," Jack said, observing the half-empty restaurant. "Must be bad for business."

"That's how it is in February and March."

"How did you know him?" Jack asked. "About the wake?"

"I saw the name in the free newspaper, that the wake was at Wah Fook. Very close by. Jun Zhang. I wasn't sure it was him."

He took a sip of tea. "How do you know him?"

"We were co-workers," she answered, *gung yau*. "At a restaurant."

"What can you tell me about him?"

"What happened to him?"

"He drowned." He spared her the details for the time being. *It wasn't exactly a lie*.

"Sad," she said. "How did it happen?"

"I was hoping you could help me with that," Jack said. He leaned in over the table.

"You mean was he depressed or something?"

"Maybe."

"He told me his name was Sing, and he was from Poon Yew village. Everyone called him Sing. He was a friendly guy." She paused. "Everyone liked him."

Not everyone, apparently, thought Jack. He knew *sing* meant "promotion" or "star" in Cantonese.

"What restaurant?" Jack followed.

"China Village," she said distantly, like it was an unwelcome memory. "Up in the *Bronxee*. Not far from the subway." Her words rang a bell in his head, fleshing out his victim now, small details slowly coming into focus.

"He made deliveries, takeout orders," she continued. "Sometimes they made him take party deliveries to the boss's house in New Jersey. He didn't like that because he lost time traveling and was losing tip money."

Always moving, Ah Por's words, Jack remembered.

"He told me he was an orphan," she said sadly. "His father was a miner who died when he was three. A mine collapsed. His mother died a year later. There was an earthquake, and they couldn't find any relatives, so they put him in the orphanage."

Jack shook his head in sympathy, encouraged her to continue.

"He said he worked in Vancouver, and Toronto, before he came to New York."

From the north, again Ah Por's words.

Their food arrived, and they continued talking through the hot-pot aromas of Southeast Asia, *pho* and *gio*.

"You mentioned that he saved you once," Jack said. "How?"

"I went on a delivery," she said. She took a breath. "There was no one else to go, and it was in the afternoon. It was already dark, but the address was close by, so they thought it would be okay."

Jack nodded for her to continue.

"When I rode past a playground, some kids chased after me. Calling me names. I became afraid they wanted more than the food." She sipped her tea. Three of them surrounded me. I stayed on the bike and dropped the delivery on the sidewalk." She shuddered. "They started grabbing at my clothes, touching me."

Jack felt rage rising from his heart to his knuckles.

"I felt so afraid," she whispered. "That's when Sing rode up and starting swinging his bicycle chain at them. Screaming like a wild man. They backed off like he was crazy, and we got away. I quit at the end of that week. But he saved me."

Jack freshened up her cup with more hot tea.

"What a shame. He had a birthday coming up. He said he wanted to see the parade, then celebrate in Chinatown."

"Parade?"

"He said his birthday was the same day as that Irish holiday. When they drink all day and have a big parade."

"Saint Patrick's Day?"

"Everyone wears green."

"Right."

"We were the same age," she said with a sigh. "Twenty-four."

Twenty-four, *yee sup say*, sounding like "easy to die" in

Cantonese. Huong looked older than twenty-four, thought Jack, probably because she'd been weathered by the outdoor elements.

"Any idea where he lived?" Jack pressed.

"No." She hesitated. "But *mox-say-go* might know."

"*Mox-say-go?*" asked Jack. *Mexican?* He tried remembering what the China Village deliveryman had said.

"Luis, he works with Cao on the big truck. They supply us from the market."

"He knows Sing?"

"They gave him a ride to Chinatown a few weeks ago. I only got a look at Sing when the truck was pulling out."

"Where is this market?" Jack asked.

"The one in the Bronxee."

"Hunts Point?"

"Sounds like that."

"Where can I find Luis now?"

"They come back down at six, to unload the vans and pack up for tomorrow."

Mexicans, the South Bronx. A crash pad somewhere.

"Do you know anything about a lighter?" he asked.

"Lighter?"

"A cigarette lighter."

She thought for a moment, finishing her *gio*. "Oh, he had a silver one. With a *say yun touh* on it."

"A skull?"

"Yes. A smiling skull."

Airborne, thought Jack. He called for the check. He'd stop by the Fifth Precinct station house for the Saint Barnabas fax, then come back for Luis.

"Do you know if he had any other problems?" he asked.

"He got robbed. He was angry about it, that the restaurant wouldn't help him."

"Gambling problems?"

"He never mentioned anything. He didn't seem like that kind of guy." A pause. "Didn't you say it was an accident?"

"I don't know that." A copspeak response.

The waiter came back and said to Jack, "Sorry, sir, it's already paid."

Jack started to protest.

"This place is my people," Huong said. "So you have to give me face. You may treat me next time, okay? But it will be at a much more *expensive* restaurant."

He had to grin at that, and accepted.

"Just find out what happened to him, Detective," she said. "He was a good person, and I pray the gods will be merciful to him." She put on her jacket, and they shook hands before she went back out into the bitter cold, to the cherries by the curb.

When he left Xe Lua, she was quickly selling fruit next to the van's gas generators, steaming in the frozen afternoon.

Fifth

COMMANDING OFFICER MARINO was reportedly attending a promotions award ceremony at headquarters. His office was empty.

Jack climbed the creaky wood steps of the Fifth Precinct, found his faxes from Saint Barnabas in a bin by the detectives' desks. The pictures of the assault victim, Dewey Lai, reminded him of some of the postmortem photos he'd developed at Ah Fook's.

The gangbanger had the requisite bruises all over his body, expected in a typical beatdown. In the gang world, nobody was nobody unless they got in a kick or two and bragged about it later. But the pictures from the emergency-admit bay of the victim's head and face were more telling. Both eyes were eggplants swollen shut—one more shut than the other. Bloody boot cuts to both sides of the head. On one side of his neck was a tattoo of the Chinese word for "dog," *gau*. On the flip side, he had a number 7 carved into his fade-style haircut, representing the seventh letter in the alphabet, G, for "Ghosts." *Another true believer.*

There was a pair of bloated fat lips on top of a swollen jaw. All the injuries of the kind that it'd take more than ten days to heal.

They would have killed him if that was their intent, Jack thought. So why? Was it just another stupid gang-boy beef? Or had Singarette owed Fay Lo's and wound up having to deal with Ghost muscle? Ex-blood brother Lucky, Ghost *dailo*, might have some answers to that, if he wasn't lying in a coma.

But maybe *dog* tattoo boy would sing, if Jack could find him.

He started making phone calls again.

By the time he left the precinct, the sky was gray. The neon colors of the restaurant signs had come to life, but there were few people on the street. He noticed a familiar figure, a woman approaching Wong's Wash n' Dry across the way.

Alexandra, he realized happily.

He crossed the street, watching Alex through the shop-window as she handed her ticket to the lady clerk. There was no one else in the shop.

He entered as the clerk disappeared behind a wall of dry-cleaning racks. Alex turned as he approached. She was pleasantly surprised.

"Heyyy," she said, smiling.

"I saw you come in," Jack said, touching her hand.

"I needed my red suit. For the legal-aid fund-raiser tonight."

He leaned in and wrapped his arms around her, felt the softness of her body against his. He savored the floral scents in her hair, took an extra *shaolin* breath.

She gave him a quick kiss, wiping the color from his lips with her fingers.

They separated as the clerk reappeared with the red suit.

"Your tickee?" the clerk asked Jack.

"*Ngo deih yat chai*," he answered. "We're *together*." He was pleased to see Alex smile at the remark.

Outside, Alex checked her watch and turned toward Mott Street. She threw a look back at Jack and mimed a phone call with her forefinger and pinkie. Jack smiled and gave her a thumbs-up.

The sky darkened after she turned the corner, and he looked toward Canal and Mulberry Streets. *Where would Huong's Mexican connection lead to?* he wondered.

Mox-Say-Go

HUONG, WHO HAD apparently explained the situation to Luis, made the introduction as they were packing up the vans. Luis was short but looked strong, like a pit bull. Jack showed his badge, assured him in his schoolboy Spanish, "*No problema. Soy policía de Nueva York. No es la inmigración.*" His words seemed to relax Luis, showing he was cool—not INS, not immigration police.

"*¿Qué quieres?*" Luis asked, climbing into the big truck.

"I need to find where he lived," Jack said.

"He stay with Ruben and Miguel."

"Where?" Jack pressed as Huong watched them from the van.

"Climb in," Luis said.

The big truck rolled north, with Jack riding shotgun, up to Hunts Point. Luis—*Luis Enriquez*—unloaded a few cases of melons to the sprawling night market, then drove them west into Mott Haven.

The place was an old building in a row of rundown tenements, a couple of blocks off the Bruckner Expressway. Jack wondered if it was one of Gooba Jai's places. *A chino-latino rent-a-bed hostel?*

They went to a second-floor apartment where one of Sing's keys fit the lock. The interior had been partitioned into smaller units, everyone sharing two little toilets and a kitchenette.

The small rooms could sleep up to three people, each on a folding cot. Luis spoke quietly to two men. They looked rugged, like they were used to hard work and long hours. Luis's explanation of Sing's demise sobered the men as Jack showed them the river photos.

"*Ay Dios mío,*" whispered Ruben. Miguel shook his head and frowned. With Luis's labored English translation and Jack's high-school Spanish, they coaxed Sing's story out of the men.

They'd been co-workers, they explained, on the Sang

Farm's trucks, delivering produce like bok choy and Chinese cabbage, mushrooms, snow peas, green onions. They pointed to Sing's cot. There was a piece of carry-on luggage underneath.

They'd known him about two months, as *Chino* more than as Sing, delivering to Chinese restaurants and markets in the Bronx. Chino was an added asset because he could speak Chinese, which sped up the deliveries.

Jack pulled out the carry-on, noticed there weren't any closets anywhere in the room. In the carry-on was an extra set of clothes—a hoodie sweatshirt, jeans, socks, a pair of sneakers. Nothing valuable. In one of the inside pockets was a bus stop map and a ticket stub.

They liked working with Sing, the men continued. He always pulled his own weight and was generous with cigarettes and food. They liked Chinese food, and he always did the ordering for them.

In a sloppy scribble on the back of the bus map were the words "edge water." No other identification, or *anything*, left behind. Jack pocketed the map and ticket stub as they gave him back the photos of Sing.

"*Hombre.*" Ruben nodded respectfully.

"When did you see him last?" Jack asked.

"*Dos noches,*" said Miguel. "Two nights ago."

"We dropped him off," added Ruben, "on a delivery."

"Delivery?" Jack asked. "For what?"

"Abba-lone-nay," Ruben enunciated, "abalone" in Spanish. "He say Chinese love it. Very expensive."

"He sold two cases," Miguel added, "and two carton cigarettes."

"Two cases of abalone?"

"*Si*, he say someone buy two cases, cash up front," said Ruben. "Sing, *Chino*, he tie a rope around each case so he can carry one in each hand."

"We dropped him off," offered Miguel. "It was only two blocks' walk. And he was supposed to meet us after, for *cerveza*."

"Where?"

"At Chino's." He hesitated. "But the real name is Booty." The word set off another bell in Jack's head. "This was what time?"

"About eight P.M.," answered Ruben, checking his watch, "like now."

"Can you drive us there?" Jack asked Luis. "I'll pay for gas and *cerveza*."

"No *problema*," Luis said.

"Sure," added Miguel. "Anything for *el chino amigo*."

THEY WENT BACK out into the night, four men in a big truck rolling west to the Highbridge section. They pulled over near a one-way street, with Booty's in the opposite direction, and dropped Jack off.

"He go down that way," Ruben said, pointing. "He say customer waiting for him by the end."

Definitely somebody was waiting, thought Jack, *maybe with a dagger in hand.* He'd given twenty dollars for *cerveza* to Luis, told them to get started at Booty's without him.

He waved them off and began walking toward the smell of water.

The growl of Luis's truck faded around a corner, *gone.* Jack continued down the street, following the dim and stranded pools of lamplight to the river. He tried to imagine Sing's thoughts and feelings as he marched through the cold, toward what might have been his last moments on earth. *I'm carrying a ten-pound case of canned abalone in each hand, using the ropes to hold each one like it was a briefcase. Also carrying two cartons of cigarettes inside a back sack.*

Hands restricted, vulnerable to attack.

The delivery has been paid for in advance. I've already made my profit, so this is just to close off the deal.

Confidence. A deceptive quality.

Then go to meet my amigos at Booty's, or Chino's, and have a few cervezas. Tomorrow's another day, right?

The long, two-block walk west to the riverfront ran through a desolate stretch of ghetto parkland.

He'd been taken completely by surprise, thought Jack. *Sing's jacket open, for a single thrust through the heart. A lucky strike? Or diligently practiced? The assailant was taller, the coroner had said.*

When Sing never shows, the Mexicans think nothing of it. They figured maybe Sing got lucky or something, shacking up elsewhere. It wasn't the first time el chino *didn't roll in until dawn.*

Gradually the streets led to a pocket park, the kind that got created by waterfront development deals and later named after politicians or city big shots. It was the early stages of gentrification butting up against the decay of the ghetto.

The little stretch of park had only six wood benches, facing the water, on land that had to be paved over anyway in order to get to the railroad tracks.

He didn't know if it was parkland or Metro North, or DOT, but the pocket park seemed public and unsecured. He noted the broken chain-link fence around a track-repair shed. You could drive a car into the area if you knew about the little back street that ran along the waterfront.

He arrived at a low railing that separated the parcel of riverside embankment from the raised concrete landing. The bank sloped off a bit, but at high tide the river would rise to the landing. *If you aren't paying attention, or if it's dark, you can walk twenty feet out and already be knee deep where the underwater bank drops off.*

Deep enough to float a body away, shove it off toward the middle of the river?

Behind him, the landing had enough space to park two or three cars, dark and distant from the solitary lamppost some fifty yards back. He heard the wind, the lapping, rippling of waves. Otherwise so quiet and deserted here that you *could* probably kill someone. *And get away with it.*

He didn't see any obvious traces of struggle or blood evidence.

He stayed there almost half an hour, trying to sort it out. Sing, the Chinese orphan from Poon Yew village, was a "paper man" who had followed a trail of established immigrant communities eastward across Canada to New York City. He came to America looking for a new future but found instead a length of steel dagger through the heart somewhere on these cold-blooded streets of the South Bronx.

Jack knew that it wasn't a random, or thrill, kill. Someone had worked it out, played the whole con, followed the hit list, and tried to *wash* it. *Someone with a purpose, a mission. Someone who'd picked the location and set up the exchange at nighttime, when it was dark and the tide was high.*

Someone who knows the area.

If it *was* just a gambling debt, then the suspicion fell on Fay Lo and the Ghosts. The Ghosts were capable of it, for sure, but it didn't seem like their style. The Ghosts were ruthless and calculated and would have simply snatched Sing off the street and left his body in a barrel somewhere. *Not some bogus abalone-and-cigarette setup in the South Bronx.*

He knew if he poked Fay Lo, he'd probably lawyer up and charge police harassment. He wasn't expecting to get a straight answer out of the Fat Man anyway.

If they *were* trying to make an example of Sing, why dispose of his body in the river? The street face of it asked, *Who collects from a dead man? Gamblers are scared off. It's bad luck, and there's a death stain on the gambling establishment.*

Jack remembered Sun Tzu's advice to strike where your opponent is weakest, and thought about *gau jai*—Ghost Doggie Boy—probably recovering somewhere in one of the Ghost crash pads in Chinatown.

IF IT WAS *more* than a gambling debt, then maybe the bad blood between Sing and Bossy Gee's restaurants figured in his murder. *Was it something he said? Something that caused one of the restaurant managers to lose face? Angry words worth dying for?*

Jack had no clue. Or rather, he had a lot of clues that didn't make sense. Like Ah Por's words, *Money is the root of all evil.*

He considered the Mexicans. Luis, Ruben, and Miguel struck him as hardworking, willing to take on dirty, low-paying jobs. In many ways, the *mox-say-gos* were the new

Chinese coolies, facing the same racist discrimination that the Chinese of earlier generations suffered. Jack could understand the reluctance to notify law enforcement. Immigrants filing police reports on other immigrants? *Not likely*, thought Jack, when they couldn't even be sure of each other's names and identities.

Nobody else ventured down the streets during the time he stayed in the pocket park. No vehicle drove by. He knew he'd have to return in daylight and check out the area again.

Daylight

IT HAD STARTED to snow, the flurries sticking to the dirt surfaces of the pocket park. Everything looked uglier in daylight, desolate and cold. Daylight alone didn't reveal any secrets. The pocket park was as deserted in daytime as it was at night.

There was no evidence mixed in with the litter that the wind had swept down from the avenue. No signs of a struggle. No telltale footprints or tire marks or bloodstains like cops always found on TV shows.

No wallet, no pack of cigarettes or lighter or scattered cans of abalone. Nothing but river debris and detritus left behind by the low tide. It'd been two nights since the Mexicans last saw Sing, and any evidence, if there'd been any, could have already washed off or blown away.

He'd have to find his clues elsewhere, and he decided to take the subway down to the Ninth Precinct, where the computer system was more updated than the Fifth's antiquated setup.

Back to the Future

His cell phone jangled as he arrived at the Ninth, signaling a voice mail that he'd missed while he was underground in the subway. He didn't recognize the number, but the message was from Alexandra, explaining that she'd be out of touch for a few days.

"Situation" was the word she used, and he understood that to mean something related to her ongoing divorce battle. The message had a tense, awkward undertone to it and ended with a curt "Call you when I get back."

When he got to the detectives' area, there were two messages with his name on them. The first one was a reminder to reschedule his appointment with the department-assigned shrink. The second was from the captain, waiting for a progress report on the John Doe now turned homicide.

Jack fired up the detectives' desktop unit and accessed the crime-file database under "Illegal Gambling and Organized Crime." The information was listed by precinct, and under Chinatown's "Fifth Precinct," he found an array of Chinese mug shots; mostly older men he didn't recognize but knew were designated sacrificial lambs whenever the vice cops were pressured to conduct a gambling raid.

Among the mug shots was an old one of Fai "Fay Lo" Yung, identified as a Chinatown businessman and associate of the On Yee tong. He had to be pushing fifty. *Eleven arrests over eight years, all of them lawyered out.* A homely man, he had a round head and a thick neck, and even though it was only a headshot, Jack could see why they'd nicknamed him Fay Lo for "fat man." All the old gambling raps on his sheet were from different locations in Chinatown, but nothing over the last five years. It was like he went underground and disappeared.

Judging from the operation in the South Bronx, Fay Lo had come a long way and had learned a thing or two about organized illegal gambling. But he was still an old-timer, from the old school that didn't believe in executing its delinquent losers. *Dead men don't pay.* They believed in making their welshers "work off" their debts by laboring for construction crews doing the nastiest jobs, or by stealing, or muling some China white or bootleg cigarettes across state lines.

The Ghosts killing Sing on their own? *A single stab through the heart?* Unlikely.

It didn't make sense.

BY THE TIME he updated the report for the captain, the winter afternoon outside looked like evening, dark already at 5 P.M. He stood up from the desk and stretched his legs, changing his stances from *tiger* to *horse* to *long bridge* squat, popping tendons and ligaments as he considered how the clues had come his way.

A cremation and a lady in red who sold cherries on a frozen street corner.

A *tres amigos* of Mexican laborers who'd pointed the way. But not the *why*.

Something personal? Or simple, like a gambling debt?

The motive escaped Jack. He planned to make more phone calls and considered enlisting Billy's help again. Although the leads had taken him in different directions, as he'd discovered on previous investigations, all roads inevitably led back to Chinatown.

Fish

JACK FOUND BILLY at Grampa's, trying to convince the part-time barmaid to visit his apartment after her shift. He complained as Jack guided him into one of the booths.

"Why is it every time I'm feeling lucky, you come along and drag me away from happiness?"

"That's not happiness, that's just sex," Jack said with a grin. "She's already wise to your game anyway."

"Well, sure, after you just cock-blocked me, whaddya expect?"

"I need your help, Billy," Jack said.

"Whoa, where have I heard that before? This is where you promise not to cum in my mouth, right?" Billy leaned back and gave Jack enough face to play out his rope. When Jack finished explaining, Billy barked, "WHAT? I hate those punk-ass Ghosts! And you want me to go down to their gambling basements?"

"Not for gambling, Billy. I want you to check it out," explained Jack. He showed him the hospital photo of Ghost Doggie Boy. "For anybody who looks like *this*."

Billy narrowed his doubtful eyes at the photo of the Ghost. "Got a tune-up. Was it something he said?"

"Should be healed up a bit. Might be wearing shades, though. And might still have a fat lip or swollen jaw."

Billy shrugged and rolled his eyes.

"What?" asked Jack.

"I could do it, but . . ."

"But *what*?"

"But," Billy began, grinning, "ain't that what they pay *you* to do?"

"You got a short memory, Bow. The last time I went down there I got suspended from the job. If I don't have a warrant, my word don't mean shit."

"So what does that make me? Like a spy? A private eye?"

"More like a CI, a confidential informant."

"Oh yeah? Sounds like a *rat*. But don't those guys get paid, somehow?"

"Yeah, you get paid in drinks here at Grampa's. And a bonus round at Angelina's, if things go right."

Billy glared at Doggie Boy's photo, staring it down like he was memorizing it.

"Okay, I'm in." Billy smirked. "Twenty bucks up front."

"What?"

"You expect me to walk around just peepin' at people and not betting? Ain't that a bit obvious?"

"Stretch it," Jack said, giving Billy the twenty.

"I wasn't planning on losing," Billy said as he finished his beer.

Jack sat in the front of the Wonton Dynasty, nursing his *gnow nom* noodles, across the street from the gambling basements on Mott. He was waiting for a call back from Billy, *CI gambling while on surveillance*.

Slurping the noodles, Jack had figured the Ghosts would still put Doggie Boy to work, earning his keep even though he was recovering. They'd have him working inside, out of sight, maybe watching the back door of one of the basements—number 55 or number 69—that the gang protected.

"Go to the back and ask for a cup of tea," Jack had advised Billy. "The drinks are always in the back."

Billy popped out of number 55 in fifteen minutes, shaking his head *no* when he spotted Jack in the noodle joint.

"No luck, boss," Billy said over the cell phone. "Seen a few scumbags. But not *that* one." He went down the block and disappeared into number 69.

Jack planned his next move as he waited.

Less than ten minutes later, Billy was back on the street, telling Jack over the cell phone, "Strike two, bro. They must've gotten this boy off the main drag."

"Go to Mulberry Street," Jack directed. "Number 79. The Video Palace is a front. Go out the back to the courtyard. They got keno and video poker there. Probably dealing cigarettes and weed, too."

"Dime bags? How much should I buy?"

"Come on, Billy!"

"Only kiddin', bro!"

"Just see if he's there," Jack groused.

"Okay, relax!" Billy snickered. "*Dewey lay*, right? If I see him, I'll call you."

Jack took a breath, recovered the Zen that Billy had drained out of him.

Let it go. Let it flow.

HE HEADED TOWARD the Harmonious Garden, walking north on Baxter Way past cop cars, prisoner vans, and corrections personnel at the monolithic Tombs facility. He greeted some of the uniformed corrections van drivers whom he'd met while signing off prisoner transfers to Rikers Island. They slapped palms as Jack continued toward the Chinese restaurant at number 99.

The Harmonious Garden was a cramped fast-food joint

that had a back door leading to a cinder-block bunker slapped up in the courtyard between buildings. The hidden bunker also led to the rear exit of 79 Mulberry Street, so gamblers could secretly walk through the block without being seen on either street.

Jack knew the On Yee *tong* covered the little operation with pocket money and probably supplied the bootleg cigarettes and whatever alcohol and drugs they were peddling. He wasn't surprised that the Ghosts ran the gambling joint under the noses of the Fifth Precinct, two blocks away, and the DOC, in the shadow of the Tombs.

The Chinese were still *invisible* to many of the uniformed, or *uninformed*, officers in the area, who mainly wanted to finish their shifts and not have to deal with the bewildering, insular Chinese community.

He ordered a quick *som bow faahn* plate, put his cell phone on the table, and kept a discreet eye on the back door. *Billy should be almost there*, he thought, sipping the hot cup of house tea the waiter had plopped down onto the plastic tabletop. He was wondering how he could get to Fay Lo without him lawyering up, when the back door swung open.

Jack watched as a gang member stepped through, wearing an oversized pair of knockoff Dolce & Gabbana sunglasses. A *short and scrawny guy*, thought Jack as the gangsta summoned a waiter and began placing orders. A punk ass with a *dailo* attitude.

The cell phone buzzed, and Jack saw Billy's message: SAW HIM. HE JUST LEFT OUT BACK.

Thanks, Jack thought sardonically, *timing is everything*. He turned his attention back to the junior gangbanger and now saw the Chinese word for "dog" tattooed on his neck.

Dropping a few dollars on the table, Jack pushed back and rose from his seat.

"Hey *gou jai!*" he called out. "Doggie Boy!" Like he was an old acquaintance.

Doggie Boy sized Jack up, sneered, and spat, "Who the fuck are you?"

Jack flapped open his jacket to flash the gold detective's shield. "Let's talk, *kai dai.*"

"Fuck you!" yelled Doggie Boy, suddenly darting out of the side door of the restaurant.

Jack sprinted after him, both of them zigzagging across Baxter Way. They were almost to the Tombs when Jack pounced and slam-tackled him into the side of a corrections van. The uniformed officers recognized Jack and prepared for backup response.

Jack twisted Doggie into an arm lock, forced him into the van.

"You make me chase you, punk *kai dai?*" Jack threw him against the wall of the van.

"What the fuck?" Doggie protested. "I didn't do nothing!"

"Then why'd you run?" Jack said as he cuffed him to the prisoner's railing.

"I got enough trouble *without* cops."

Jack pulled a switchblade out of Doggie's jacket. "Well, now you got *more* trouble coming," Jack threatened.

"Fuck you! I didn't—" Doggie cursed as Jack bitch-slapped him across the face, sending the fake D&G shades flying and revealing the bruises still evident around Doggie's eyes.

"Owwww fuck!" Doggie howled.

Jack braced him against the prisoner bench and showed him the river photo of dead Sing.

"Oh shit!" Doggie cursed, shaking his head. "What the fuck is that?"

"He owed Fay Lo," Jack said. "And you punk asses killed him when he couldn't pay up!"

"What? No, man! You got that shit all wrong!"

"You suckered him and killed him!"

"No, man! Thass *crazy*! Who da fuck collects from a dead man?"

"Yeah, you were trying to make an example out of him."

"Thass crazy, yo! Swear to God, we didn't have nothing to do with killing him!"

"*Who* did then?"

"How the fuck should I know?"

"Look, *boy*. You keep boo-shitting me, and I don't have the time to waste. We're already here at the Tombs. See my brothers outside? They can process you quick, get you off to Rikers."

"Naw, man. No way. I didn't do nothing!"

"Yeah, *you*. And your Ghost punks."

"No way!" Doggie continued protesting. "Thass crazy."

"I'm going to charge you with promoting and protecting an illegal gambling enterprise," Jack said, stone-faced. "And weapons possession for the stiletto. Then I'm going to bust the blockhouse and tell them *you* gave it up, and we had to arrest you just to make it look good. Gonna tell them you're my snitch now, okay, bitch? How you think that's going to play? And you probably got priors and probation and whatever other shit you got on your sheet that will put you on the express back to Rikers anyway. You know how the brothers there will welcome your tight little Chinese ass, right?"

Jack's last sentence seemed to get Doggie Boy's attention.

"But I didn't do nothing," he started to whine.

"Right. You caught a beating for nothing outside Fay Lo's. I know who did it," Jack bluffed. "But here's your chance to tell your side—why they tuned you up." Jack pointed to the uniformed guards on the street. "Or I turn you over to *them*."

Jack paused, pushed open the van door, and turned to leave. "Last chance," he offered, watching Doggie's eyes glaze over for what seemed like forever.

"All right!" Doggie yelled bitterly before surrendering what the rival gang boys had beaten out of him.

"The guy was into Fay Lo for five K," he began. "Mostly from card games. They knew he worked at one of Bossy Gee's restaurants and knew he was mad at Bossy's people."

"Go on."

"He delivered to Bossy's house and knew the location. So Fay Lo washed the debt in exchange for the address."

"Why Bossy's address?"

"I don't know."

Kidnap, arson, robbery, or murder? wondered Jack. "What's the address?"

"I don't know."

"Don't bullshit me, boy!" Jack barked. "Bossy's boys tuned you up for something you didn't know?"

"They wanted to know *how* we knew the address."

"And you gave Sing up."

Doggie nodded. "They wouldn't stop beating me!"

"You got him killed," said Jack.

"He got himself killed!"

"So what happened? You went to the house . . ."

"Not me! I don't have the rank for that. Only the *dailos*."
He took a quick, hard breath. "Fuck! First I get beat by those
Dragon faggots, now I get beat by the cops!"

"I *never* beat you, punk. You called me 'fuck' one time too
many, that's why you got slapped. You can't take a bitch-slap,
you better get the fuck out of the bad-boy business."

"All bool-shit! That's all I got," Doggie said. "So charge
me or let me call the lawyer. No fears!"

*Bossy or his people—probably the Dragons, who were arch
enemies of the Ghosts anyway—killed Sing as some kind of
payback*, figured Jack. *But payback for what?* He stared
down Doggie Boy, thinking, *Charge him now and arrest
him for illegal gambling, but open a pool of worms on Chinatown organized crime and confidential informants. And
attract an Internal Affairs investigation into possible police
misconduct.*

Or play catch and release? Throw Doggie back into the
swamp. Pull him out whenever needed. A snitch. A born-to-
be bitch. A fish.

Ghost *dailo* Lucky wasn't any help anymore, thought
Jack, but now he had another confidential informant to
work on, a low-level, street-rank 49. A *say gou jai*, dead dog,
in the Ghost Legion.

Jack decided to release him.

"It's your lucky night, punk!" Jack uncuffed Doggie and
booted him out of the van. "Your takeout should be ready
now!" he called out, watching Doggie shuffle off back toward
the Harmonious Garden.

A fish in a barrel.

The Tombs guards allowed Jack the use of their internal
directory, and the first call went as he expected: the night

operator at Edgewater PD informed him that shift detectives were out in the field, but if it was an *emergency*, she might be able to patch through a message.

Jack left his number, said he'd be in Edgewater in the morning.

He checked the time, figured it wasn't too late to be calling Vincent Chin.

O. G.

THE MORNING BROUGHT Jack back to the side streets behind the Tombs facility. He was looking for Vincent Chin, editor of the *United National*, Chinatown's oldest Chinese-language newspaper. Vincent had assisted Jack on previous Chinatown cases by providing not only what was fit to print but also neighborhood gossip, street talk, and unsubstantiated chatter from old women and shiftless men in smoky coffee shops.

The *United National* was Chinatown's *hometown* paper and had been Pa's favorite.

Jack followed the streets leading into TriBeCa, the gentrified "triangle" of streets below the Canal Street thoroughfare. He'd brought along two containers of *nai cha* tea from Eddie's.

The *National* was located in a renovated storefront on White Street across from the Men's Mission and was the only Chinatown newspaper without a color section. The pressmen still typeset by hand the thousands of Chinese characters needed to go to print.

Vincent, who looked younger than his forty years, was in

the copy room reviewing what the pressmen had laid out when Jack walked in.

"In my office," Vincent said. "I'll be a few minutes."

A SMALL OFFICE, but on the editorial desk along the wall, Vincent had laid out an array of Chinese news articles, arranged in a loose chronological order, featuring Bossy *Jook Mun* Gee and his family.

Jack couldn't read all the Chinese words, but he scanned the accompanying photographs and could figure out what the story was about. Everything in black and white, Cantonese block characters like ideographs.

The first news article, in a "Profiles" piece, was a full-page historical perspective on three generations of a prominent family.

The Gees.

The Gees were an old-line Chinatown family, dating their presence in New York City to 1925, to the remnants of the *bachelor generation*. There was a posed studio photo of the *patriarch*, Gee Duck Hong, with floral accents and a Chinese landscape in the background.

Old man Gee started Dynasty Noodles, which became the largest Chinese pasta manufacturing company on the East Coast. Expanded the *gwai lo* taste for lo mein, chow mein, and wonton noodles. A Gum Shan, a mountain of noodles.

There was a photo of Bossy *Jook Mun* Gee, who'd been promoted to director at Dynasty Noodles, and in a separate photo with his young sons, Gary and Francis, attending local *gifted* schools.

Jack smiled. *Three generations of a successful, assimilated Chinese American family*.

"What the article doesn't mention," Vincent said, coming into the closet office, "is that the old man Gee Duck was in bed with the Hip Ching Association and had his greedy fingers big time in paper identities and illegal alcohol and untaxed cigarettes."

"Good morning." Jack grinned.

"Morning." Vincent smiled. "The old man had Triad connections with the Hok Nam Moon in Toishan, and to an import-export company that tied him to the opium and heroin trade."

"Nice guy," Jack said.

"The article doesn't mention his arrests for bookmaking, extortion, and gambling rackets. All before my time," Vincent said. "In 1950, his partner in Dynasty Noodles died mysteriously while on a trip to Taiwan—something about a traffic accident and a heart attack."

Jack took a sip of his *nai cha*. Bossy was known to be a backer of the Hip Ching gambling dens, Chinatown liquor stores, and dry-goods companies he could manipulate to smuggle contraband.

The Chinatown buildings the old man bought, with the backing of the Gee Association, when nobody wanted them back in the 1930s, were now worth untold millions. Vincent added, after taking a moment to add brown sugar to his tea, "They have an office on Pell Street. Manage all the real estate and businesses there."

The second article included a photo of a younger Bossy, maybe fortyish, smiling on a pristine lot of land in Edgewater, New Jersey, not far from the Yaohan Plaza Japanese sushi mall on the waterfront.

It was an architectural feature, translated from *Design*

Digest magazine. Bossy *James* Gee was planning a large reno-vation of his house to accommodate an extended immigrant family. The article featured a rendering of the house with all the latest gadgets and accoutrements: a koi garden inside a security perimeter, a two-car garage, a satellite dish, an out-door pool with a hot tub.

His sons looked older in the accompanying photo. *Teen-agers?* One much taller than the other. Standing off in the distance. Dad, doing all the posing, and talking for them all.

A modern family in a suburban setting.

There was no mention of the actual address of the site, but a traffic sign in the photo showed its proximity to Yaohan Plaza.

Attached was a little follow-up article on complaints from longtime residents of Edgewater about Asians building "monster homes" in the area. Bossy's neighbors, citing con-struction noise and inconveniences and traffic problems, complained that the large, three-level houses were ostenta-tious and detracted from the "rustic simplicity" of the neighborhood.

"Same thing happened in Vancouver and Toronto. And other places," said Vincent. "Wealthy Chinese immigrants arrive in a formerly all-white area. They buy a house, tear it down. Then they build a giant multilevel house on the plot, to the resentment of the neighbors." He blew the steam off his tea. "Hey, Asians have big families, right? But it's caused big problems. Whole Chinese communities have been uprooted in the face of what some consider racism and moved to more isolated but friendlier locations."

The fourth piece was an investigative report on surveil-lance operations conducted by the OCCB—the Organized

Crime Control Bureau—focusing on Jook Mun "James" Gee as a member of the Hip Ching *tong*, being investigated for illegal gambling, smuggling contraband, and affiliation with the notorious Chinatown Black Dragons street gang. Possible ATF investigation. The Hip Chings themselves were targets of a federal probe into RICO—Racketeering Influenced Corrupt Organizations—activities.

Bossy had hired Solomon Schwartz, one of the top criminal defense lawyers in the city. There were no indictments. Schwartz got "circumstantial evidence" dismissed at that point.

"They nicknamed him 'Bossy,'" Vincent continued, "because of the way he liked to order people around. Bossy Gee, only son of the legendary Gee Duck Hong. Fifteen years ago he was accused of hiring an underaged Chinese girl for a massage, and then molesting her. The teenager wanted to press charges, but her mother stopped her, and the case was settled out of court."

Did Bossy pay off the family, or threaten them?

"Rumor has it that Bossy's wife wanted a divorce," Vincent said. "But he refused. Eventually she moved back to family in Taiwan. Guess she felt that she'd lost face and didn't wanted to hear Chinatown gossip."

Two small news items were taped together. One featured an honor guard of old Chinese veterans from the local American Legion Post placing a wreath at the Kimlau Gate on Memorial Day, honoring Chinatown's war dead. The other item was a mention of a military funeral proceeding out of the Wah Fook parlor. A photo of Marines in parade dress uniforms, shouldering the flag-draped coffin of "Gary" *Ying Hong* Gee, on Mulberry Street. Another photo showing Gary posing proudly in uniform.

Both men were quiet for a moment as they sipped their teas.

"The story is that Gary Gee wanted to serve his country and then use the GI Bill to go to college. He wanted to study law, wanted to make a difference. He wanted to earn it on his own, not use his father's Chinatown influence. Joining the Marines seemed like a good choice." Jack knew what Vincent meant. Despite a few global hot spots, it had been a peacetime military, with the United States patrolling the world.

"Gary was the tangerine of his father's eye," Vincent added. "But almost at the end of his tour, there was a Hezbollah truck-bomb attack on a Marine barracks. You probably remember, it was in the Middle East. Twelve thousand pounds of TNT killed about two hundred Marines. Gary was one of them."

They stared at the photo of the military funeral outside the Wah Fook.

"His father and grandfather were devastated, mourning the death of their favorite child. They had twenty-five cars in the funeral cortege. Younger brother Frank went along but didn't hide his displeasure at being forced to go to the cemetery. He got into a fight with a photographer from one of the other dailies." There was a small photo of Frank, a scowling juvenile face, fists clenched and cocked at the camera.

Jack imagined the casket being lowered into the ground, a soldier trumpeting taps in the background.

"The old man, Duck Hong, died a couple of months ago." Vincent frowned. "He had a heart attack at home. Not many details, just an obituary. Apparently they handled it all in New Jersey."

"They didn't want to publicize a natural death?" Jack said, guessing aloud.

Vincent shrugged, didn't have an answer.

After a run of bad press, is Bossy just trying to stay out of the limelight? Jack wondered. *Just trying to run his business low key?* Was there more to the story? *Money*—he heard Ah Por's whisper again—*evil*. He swept the news items and photos into a folder and pocketed them inside his jacket.

Jack thanked Vincent, and they agreed to do *dim sum* sometime. He knew Vincent would appreciate an inside scoop when the case got resolved.

Taking the side streets back into Chinatown, Jack headed for Pell Street, where the Hip Ching ruled, with the vicious muscle of the Black Dragons. Looking for a prominent man from a powerful Chinatown family, and for answers to questions still floating in the frigid morning.

THE FIVE-STORY, BROWN-BRICK building at the corner of Mott and Pell was one of the few that still featured Chinese roof architecture, curved tiles that resembled lengths of green bamboo on a slanted, pagoda-style façade.

A Baskin-Robbins ice cream shop occupied the large storefront on Mott, but the building's entrance was at 36 Pell.

The second-floor apartments had all been converted to commercial offices featuring large picture windows that overlooked the busy corner. Signs in the windows promoted a Hong Kong travel agency, an immigration lawyer, an accountant, and a real-estate broker.

Jack wondered if the Hip Chings owned the building. Many of the Chinatown *tongs* and family associations had a history of purchasing buildings on the same street where their clan headquarters were located. In Depression-era New York City, many white building owners desperately sought to liquidate their holdings to reduce landlord liabilities, and in turn, the Chinatown Chinese snapped up whatever properties they could.

Jack also wondered if Bossy Gee, a Hip Ching crony, owned a piece of the building.

He stepped into number 36 and scanned the office listings posted on the wall.

Bossy's company, Golden Mountain Realty, was away from the window offices out front, but was the first room off the short flight of stairs. Gold plastic letters, GOLDEN MOUNTAIN REALTY, gleamed above the entrance.

The industrial-gray door was a neat piece of hardware—solid steel with a top half-panel of thick glass, heavy-duty locks and door handle—the kind of door you'd expect at a ghetto check-cashing place, not a Chinatown realty office.

The other doors on the landing were pushovers by comparison.

He pressed the door button and waited. He noticed the surveillance camera, high over his left shoulder in the far corner of the window wall. *Covers all the businesses and residents' comings and goings.* On the other side of the glass panel was a reception area, a pretty lady behind a desk with a computer screen and phone-fax setup. She looked to be in her thirties, was probably older but still kept herself looking good. Business jacket, professional look.

She buzzed him in.

Jack badged her right away. She seemed to be alone in the office, and he wanted to put her at ease. "I need to speak with Mr. Gee," Jack said, glancing at the open door to an empty inner office. The place had a new-car smell.

"He's not here today," she answered in her smiling Hong Kong Cantonese. "But I can try to call him. What is this about, *ah sir*?"

"Just tell him it's a *police* matter." Jack smiled politely as she gestured toward one of the quilted black leather chairs. *Knockoffs from China*, he thought. He sat down, scanning the office as she made the call. There were real-estate postings on the walls, photos of various buildings in Chinatown and other locations in the Tri-State area. Commercial as well as residential properties. Most of the listings centered near Chinese or Asian communities—Chinatowns, K-Towns and J-Towns, Little Saigon/Malaysia/Bombay, etc. There was a long counter on the wall behind him where the realty sections from various Chinese-language newspapers featured their own listings and properties.

One of the listings was a luxury home in Edgewater, New Jersey: 88 Edgewater Lane.

"I'm sorry," she said. "He's not picking up. He may be in the field." She sounded like she'd practiced the line.

"Could you try once more?" Jack asked, nodding his *thank you* as she tried the call again. He wondered if she was being loyal to her boss, *Bossy Gee*, and was just playing him, the *chaai lo*. He tried to recall Singarette's notation on the New Jersey bus map.

She let her call continue for a full minute before announcing, "He's still not picking up. Sorry."

"Can you try his cell phone?"

She called, but after a few seconds said, "It's going to voice mail."

Jack extended his NYPD detective's card to her.

"Please have him call me," he said.

"*Ho ahh.*" She smiled. "Certainly."

She buzzed him out, and as he stepped back through the heavy door, he felt like he'd beaten lockdown at Rikers.

She was still smiling at him as he turned away from the hallway camera and walked down the stairs to Pell Street.

Outside the Fifth Precinct on Elizabeth Alley, he looked for the undercover cars and found an old Chevy Impala, its NYPD parking placard visible on the dash.

The sergeant at the duty desk didn't recognize him at first and continued reviewing the assignments on his roster as he gave Jack another once-over.

"The Chevy's with Fields and Malone," he said finally, tossing Jack the car keys. "They're in court until the end of the shift."

"I'll have it back before then," Jack promised. "Thanks."

He ran the engine a few minutes, letting the Impala warm up before heading for the West Side Highway toward the George Washington Bridge. The GWB would take him across the Hudson into Fort Lee, New Jersey.

He didn't know the area well but figured he could find Edgewater directly, since it was part of the same county.

On the Edge

He kept the frosted bathroom lights off. There was enough daylight from the vent windows, he felt.

The coolness of the marble floor curled around his ankles.

He ran the shiny brass faucet for a few seconds, catching a dim glimpse of himself in the mirror, before cupping the warm water in his hands and bringing it to his face. The rinse felt welcoming, *purifying*. Some of the splash left wet blotches on the sleeves of his blue Ascot Chang bathrobe.

He didn't care.

His vision was blurred by the second and third rinse, and it took him a minute to refocus on the face in the mirror. Except for the puffiness under his eyes, he decided he didn't look too bad for a man whose next milestone birthday would make him sixty years old, five cycles of the Chinese horoscope.

Nobody is guaranteed six cycles, he thought, especially considering all the trouble he'd had in recent years.

He smoothed the excess water from his hands into his hair, roughly combing it back with his fingers. He patted his face dry and left the towel by the side of the polished stone sink, remembering that he'd canceled the cleaning woman's contract two weeks earlier because it didn't matter anymore.

He'd decided to move out. The only question was where.

He padded quietly, in his soft Jimmy Choo slippers, through the silence in the big empty house, past the rare jade vases and the classical Chinese calligraphy framed and hanging on the pearly walls, down the thickly carpeted steps, and around to the modern walk-through kitchen, where he powered up the small TV on the counter, already set to the Chinese cable channel. *Just to have some noise in the house*. Made it feel like he wasn't alone.

HE POURED HIMSELF a shot of XO and tried to remember which days they'd lined up for showing the house.

He was pleased to be using his own realty company, thereby cutting costs dramatically, and trusted the veteran agents to whom he'd given the exclusives to sell what was where he and his family had lived the last fifteen years of his life. *A lot of history, good and bad.*

The tri-level house had been silent since his father's funeral, since his mother and wife returned to Hong Kong and Taiwan, respectively. Franky, his son, hadn't been home in days, which wasn't unusual.

"James" *Jook Mun* Gee, businessman and entrepreneur, knew he didn't need the house anymore. What was once a social statement was now just a bad memory, where bad things had taken place, and where bad feelings still lingered in the air.

He downed the XO and poured another.

He considered his other places in Virginia and Pennsylvania. Not too far from New York City. Nice, two-family-type homes he could relocate to. Big enough for the extended family from overseas. But he knew Franky would never go.

He'd be alone most of the time.

In the end, he didn't really want to leave New York City. Too many opportunities and, besides, his Hip Ching and Triad associations were all in the city.

He'd been considering condominiums in Sunset Park, the Brooklyn Chinatown, or on the outskirts of the Flushing, Queens, Chinatown. *Places where he can blend in.* He pulled a Cuban cigar from a crevice in an intricately carved ivory tusk, engraved with the legends of the Five Villages.

He fired up the cigar, no longer expecting a wife's complaint about the smell.

The realty agents all carried air freshener, he knew.

Sell the house, he focused. He'd make an easy half-million profit in the sale anyway. Next, move to smaller digs. Allow for his estranged wife and his wayward son, Franky, but not let them limit him. *A condo in Manhattan?* The women would like that. *Better values in Brooklyn?* He knew Franky wouldn't give a shit whatsoever.

Somewhere he could start anew?

He kept having the flashbacks.

He'd wanted to retreat to one of the other homes, but conditions were *inappropriate*. He'd alerted his agents in Brooklyn. Not far from Manhattan, with easy access.

He didn't want to live in the house much longer.

And the flashbacks just made things worse.

THE IMPALA HELD its own on the highway, and Jack could see the GWB in the distance. He wondered about the old man, Bossy's father, Gee Duck Hong, and what his life must have been like. As a younger man he would have been a prominent member of the bachelor generation in Chinatown—Jack's father's generation—when Chinese bachelors satisfied their needs with alcohol, opium, gambling, and prostitutes in an atmosphere of organized *tong* crime and racial discrimination. It was a time when Chinese hatchet men fought each other with meat cleavers and hammers on Doyers Street, and along Mott and Pell; men who had never before wielded a knife or tool in anger learned quickly from the *gwai lo* whites, vicious gangs like the Dead Rabbits, the Bowery Boys. This was Gee Duck Hong's time. Pioneering times, and tribalism, for the Chinese in New York City. Wealthy merchants shunned the lowly laundrymen and street vendors as class struggle laid bare the conflicting internal politics of Chinatown, even as the community was fighting for its very life against municipal corruption and racism.

Pa's history lesson faded in Jack's brain as the old Chevy crossed the bridge and brought him into Fort Lee.

He drove through upscale bedroom communities with stately homes in the million-dollar range, surrounded by tall, hardy trees, natural vistas, a nearby lakefront. He cranked down the window and caught the rich scent of old money in the rush of cold air.

There was still some snow cover, not unusual at the higher elevation, with chunks of frozen slush shoveled to the curbside. He passed rows of bare hedges, graveled driveways, and finally found the street that led to the Edgewater station house. Soon enough, he came to a modern brick facility with multipurpose trailers forming a perimeter. There was plenty of open parking in a back lot, but Jack parked the Chevy as close as he could get to the main entrance.

THE DETECTIVE ON duty seemed to be waiting for him, a beefy guy with ruddy cheeks in a rumpled suit. He had a salt-and-pepper military haircut. Jack wondered if he'd just come in from the cold, imagining him in the woods in camouflage gear, bow hunting deer or blowing away a bear with an assault rifle.

Jack broke the awkward quiet by placing his ID and gold shield on the duty desk.

"So what's up, *brother?*" the Jersey detective greeted Jack, direct but accommodating, while pointing toward one of the metal folding chairs. He took another look at Jack's ID and badge, apparently having never met, much less ever having had a conversation with, a Chinese cop, NYPD, federal, or otherwise.

"I'm working a homicide," Jack began in his perfect Lower East Side English, "which could be connected to something that might've happened out here."

"*Might* have happened?" The Edgewater cop seemed pleasantly surprised by Jack's command of the language.

"Something like kidnap, burglary, robbery. Or home invasion, arson?"

"Out *here?*" The crew cut narrowed his eyes. He was reviewing local crimes in his head.

"In Edgewater. Could be tied to a Mr. James Gee." Jack added, "A big house. I don't have an address." He thought he saw the man blink on *Gee.*

"This was *how* long ago?"

"Has to be recent," Jack offered. "A few weeks, coupla months maybe."

There was a long pause as the two men sat back, sizing each other up. *You have a lot of that out here*, wondered Jack during the delay, *or hardly any? A crime happens just across the river, in another state, but unless it's a notorious case with a federal tie-in, he'd never hear about it.*

"You're right. There *was* a home invasion," the Jersey cop finally offered, like it was bait. "In February. What now? You got a *lead* for me?"

"Not yet," Jack countered, "but I got a victim who maybe died because of it. Your home invasion had Chinese victims?"

"We don't record data based on race."

"I know that." Jack shrugged, working the cop-brother angle. "Just off the record, anything with a James Gee?"

The crew cut took another long breath. "Okay," he said. "But anything you get comes my way. Gang intel, organized crime, immigration. *Everything.*" Color rose on his face.

"You got it," Jack said.

"It's the only open case in my jacket," he said frowning. "And anybody who comes and fucks around in *my* backyard, they gotta pay. Whether the victim helps us or not."

"How's that?"

"The victim, Mr. Gee—it wasn't 'James' as I remember, something else Chinese—was cooperative but didn't give us anything really useful. I got the idea he knew more than he was telling."

"Go on."

"Gee said he had no enemies that he knew of and was unaware of any threats against him or his family. We later thought it might have something to do with his son Francis, who had two criminal mischief and grand theft auto beefs here. We didn't get anywhere with that."

"How'd it go down? The home invasion?"

"Patrol got the call, a nine-eleven," he said, "during the change of shift. A resident of Edgewater Lane complained that a car had sideswiped him at high speed as he was pulling in outside his home. He claimed the car came from the direction of Mr. Gee's house."

"He knew the location of Mr. Gee's house?" Jack asked.

"He said 'the *Chinaman's* house.'" The crew cut watched for a reaction from Jack.

Nothing but his inscrutable face.

He continued the tale.

"So patrol went to the location. Some lights were on inside the house. No one answered the front door, but the side doors were open. They found Mr. Gee and his father inside. Both were bound and gagged. Gee had a gash on the back of his head, nothing serious, and the old man complained about chest pains. They put out a call for EMS."

"How many perps? How'd they gain access?"

"Mr. Gee said he had a security alarm system but hadn't activated it for the night, as he thought his son might be coming home late. He said the alarms in the area had activated last year during the nor'easter, and again when we had the tremors in the Palisades. They had to wait a long time for the alarm company to respond. So he kept the system off until they were ready to sleep. Most of the time he said it was just him and his father. That night, three armed men surprised them."

"What happened to the old man?" Jack remembered Vincent Chin's words, *natural death*.

"He had a massive stroke before EMS arrived. They pronounced him at the hospital."

"What about the son?" Jack asked.

"Wasn't home. Was at a party, and the alibi's good."

Jack shook his head. "He had nothing to say?"

"Again, nothing that was helpful. But not surprising, since he's on probation here."

"Probation? You got him on a leash?"

"Yeah, but he hasn't violated, as far as we know."

Jack remembered the house mentioned in the architecture magazine.

"What's the address?" he asked, wondering if Bossy Gee was at home.

Flash-Forward

He avoided the living room, only glancing around it in passing. He'd wiped away the streaks of blood from his head gash that had smeared against the couch and carpet. The luxurious leather furniture combination, arranged in a *feng shui* pattern, was still as pristine as ever. No prospective buyer could possibly know that the old man died there, on the carpet, next to the ottoman.

His father, bound hands and feet, choking inside his duct-taped mouth. The memory froze him breathless.

Terror in the old man's eyes.

He poured another shot of XO.

Three men in ski masks, brandishing guns and knives, had gotten the drop on them.

Snubbed out the Cubano cigar.

They'd pistol-whipped him and taken cash and jewelry.

He took the rest of the alcohol back up to the bedrooms, trying to shake the flashbacks.

Somehow, the police arrived, freeing them. Suffering the loss of face, the humiliation.

He viewed the front of his property through the large picture windows. Downed the XO. *I can't stay here much longer*, he knew. There was going to be some more payback coming, and he didn't intend to be a sitting duck here. He needed to be *very* low-key. *Disappear*, and let the Hong Kong Triad do its work. He'd want to keep his remaining son, Frank, out of harm's way, but he'd sponsor the Black Dragons to continue hitting the Ghosts wherever they spread to.

The lakeside trees were bare, but the evergreens still framed the house in green and lined the driveway approach.

He took a long breath and found calm again. A fresh brushing of snow had covered over the gray slush, and everything looked picturesque. The sales agents had posted a sign at the beginning of the driveway.

In the distance a car turned onto the lane, slowing as it passed the other houses. He tried to remember if they were showing the house today.

The car came to a stop at the driveway, idling opposite the FOR SALE sign, spitting little puffs of steamy exhaust from its tailpipe. *Is it a prospective buyer coming for a look at the house?* he wondered. *Or someone who's lost trying to circle back to the highway?* He waited for some movement from the car.

JACK SAT BACK in the Chevy and admired the big house at the far end of the fancy white-gravel driveway. The FOR SALE sign presented 88 Edgewater Lane, an offering by Golden Mountain Realty. *The biggest house in the neighborhood, fronted by the luckiest Chinese numbers*, thought Jack, *three levels tall. A long, private driveway. Roof deck. Probably has a pool and a hot tub out back.* He remembered the "monster homes" news item and wondered how one man's American Dream had ended in a fatal home invasion.

AFTER ABOUT FIVE minutes, the car nosed into the driveway. He half expected it to reverse back into a U-turn, but it rolled slowly toward the house. As it came closer he could see that it was an old car, a beat-up junker, not the type of vehicle usually seen on the rich side of Edgewater.

It stopped well short of the house. The little puffs of

steam stopped streaming from its rear, and he knew the driver had killed the engine.

He resisted the urge to bring his chromed nine millimeter out of the armoire drawer. *No one is going to get the drop on me again.* He put the alcohol down on the dresser, watched the car from behind the curtains. A man got out and crunched his way across the gravel to his front door. A *Chinese* man in a parka, who struck him somehow as being American born, a *jook sing.* The man looked around covertly as he rang the doorbell.

JACK WAITED WHILE the door chime rang out a melodious tune. Waited another minute before hitting it again. Knocked on the door forcefully.

"NYPD," Jack heard himself announcing. "I'm here to speak with Gee *saang,* Mr. Gee." As far as he could tell, there were no lights on in the house. No cars in the driveway. He waited and weighed checking the sides and rear of the house.

MAAT LUN SI ah? he wondered. *What the fuck? A New York cop in Jersey?*

Everything was locked down, the alarm company on point ever since the *invasion.* The Chinese *chaai lo* cop was tripping the motion detectors, was being recorded on the surveillance setup.

He kept quiet and continued to watch from behind the curtains.

IT DIDN'T SEEM like anyone was home, and Jack didn't want to set off any alarms on the property or in Bossy's head.

Playing by the book, he backed off to what he thought was the property line and observed what he could. *A path to the lake area behind the house. No vehicles anywhere. A patio area that looks unused. Apparently no one home.*

THE PHONE SOUNDED somewhere in the bedroom. He found it under one of the pillows and recognized his office number calling. He hoped the cop hadn't heard it.

"*Maatsi?*" he asked his receptionist. "What's the matter?"

"You had a visitor," she answered. "A *chaai lo.*"

"Yes." He knew. *He's outside now.*

"He left his card, asked that you call him."

He thought for a moment, saw the Chinese cop circling to the far side of the house. "Call him back *now*," he instructed, "and tell him I'll be in the office in two hours." He had no intention of letting him into the house.

"*Ho ah*," she acknowledged and hung up.

He rushed to Franky's room to get a better angle. He saw the cop pull a phone from his jacket. The conversation was short, and the cop took a last look at the house before turning back toward the junker in driveway.

JACK GOT BACK in the Impala, fired it up while replaying the receptionist's words in his head. Two hours was plenty of time to get back to Bossy's office, but he knew now there were more answers in Chinatown than in New Jersey.

He wondered about the receptionist and why Bossy'd hired a mature woman instead of some young tart eye candy, which many Chinatown offices featured. She acted like she'd worked there awhile, and Jack thought maybe she was loyal to him, *protective*.

He had time enough for a quick *som bow faahn* when he got back to Chinatown, and a few words with Billy Bow.

The car spat steam again as it crunched gravel back toward the highway.

Franky Noodles

THE NOISE LEVEL in Eddie's was amped, and they both leaned in over their *Three Precious* plates of rice, *som bow faahn*, to hear each other.

"*Francis* Gee?" Billy grinned. "Really?"

Jack nodded as he forked up a piece of soy-sauce chicken.

"Everybody in Chinatown calls him 'Franky Noodles,'" Billy continued. "Hangs with the Black Dragons. He ain't no fighter; he's a rich-boy wannabe. Daddy's got some juice." He jabbed up a piece of *for ngaap*, roast duck.

"The Dragons still working out of that spot behind Half-Ass?" Jack asked, working a forkful of *cha siew*, roast pork, and fried egg.

"Yeah. I hate those motherfuckers as much as I hate the Ghosts, you know?"

"Yeah," Jack agreed, knowing Billy hated the thugs and gang culture ruling Chinatown. "He got any beefs?"

"The usual shit between the Dragons and Ghosts. But he's a player," Billy sneered. "Drives a tricked-out red Camaro. Acts tough because he knows Daddy can bail him out."

"Sounds like you don't like him, man."

"I hate them *all*." Billy chomped a chunk of *for yook*. "Punk asses giving us hardworking Chinamen a bad name."

"Right," Jack agreed, thinking about Half-Ass restaurant and Franky Noodles on Hip Ching–controlled Pell Street. "You got that right."

THE RECEPTIONIST AT Golden Mountain buzzed Jack in and stalled him while she announced him over the phone intercom. The door to the inner office was open, and he saw a big desk and a pair of club chairs inside.

He took a brochure that had a smiling thumbnail shot of James Gee *saang* and a business card from the tray on her desk.

She waved him in, rising from her secretarial seat.

Once inside, Jack saw how small the office actually was. James Gee stood to one side of the carved Chinese desk. He was as tall as Jack but had a thick build, thirty pounds overweight made to look neat in the expensive gray suit. Jack suspected his shirt and shoes came with designer labels attached as well, a CEO power-meeting getup straight out of businessmen's *GQ*.

Jack noticed how he combed his short hair straight back, old-school style, the way the Chinese barbers on Doyers Street still cut hair.

The door closed behind him as "James" *Jook Mun* spoke first. "*Chor,*" he said imperiously in smooth Cantonese, "have a seat," motioning in the direction of the club chairs. He wore a haggard edge beneath his eyes that his smile didn't soften.

Jack imagined the faint scent of whiskey and cigars in the air as he sat, quickly scanning the room. There was minimal decor, just a few low file cabinets lining one wall, above which were some framed photos of James with other Chinese men posing with Fraternal Order of Police organizations.

The wall behind the desk featured awards and photos of Chinatown civic groups, a plaque from the Senior Citizens' Free Breakfast Program, a miniature American flag. He didn't see any family photos at all.

"Mr. Gee," Jack began, wanting to start off respectfully before he got to the hard questions.

"Before we begin, Detective," James interrupted, "there's something I'm curious about, that I'd like to ask you first."

"Sure," Jack said agreeably. "Go ahead."

"My police friends are much older than you," James began, "closer to retiring. A few of them have inquired about security positions in our commercial buildings."

Jack nodded politely, let him continue.

"The problem is, most of the businesses are Chinese, and these policemen are *not*. Nor do they speak Chinese. I don't think the tenants can be happy with that." He paused, sized Jack up with a curious look.

"You said you had a question," Jack said.

"I was wondering if someone like yourself might consider a security manager position? There aren't many Chinese policemen, and we both know the pay could be better."

"I'm happy where I'm at right now," answered Jack with a small smile. "Someday, maybe, but thanks for the consideration." *Friendly enough so far*, he thought.

James held his smile, but something calculating flashed in his eyes.

Jack sensed that they were like two boxers—martial artists—feeling each other out, circling and measuring before throwing punches. He reached into his jacket and took out the snapshot of Singarette, dead in the river. He slid it across the desk and watched it nail James's attention.

James stared at it a moment before picking it up.

"I'm investigating the death of Jun Wah Zhang," Jack said.

James said nothing, waiting for the rest of it, with the frozen smile on his face.

"Know him?" Jack asked.

"No." James frowned.

"Never seen him?" pressed Jack.

"Never." He slid the snapshot back to Jack, shook his head. "It's sad when people die."

Jack nodded his agreement, adding, "He worked at one of your restaurants."

"That may be," James acknowledged. "But I don't know *all* the workers in *all* my businesses. There must be hundreds."

"He may have had problems in your restaurants," Jack added.

"I have no idea about that," James said coolly. "I leave that to the managers." He flashed his Cheshire Cat grin again. *Like he knew it'd come to nothing,* thought Jack. *If anything, he'd throw one of the managers under the bus.*

"So you have no idea what might have led to his death, Gee *saang?*"

"Absolutely no idea."

Both men took a breath at the pause.

"Where were you four nights ago, Gee *saang?*" Jack asked abruptly, "between eight and ten P.M.?"

An incredulous look froze James's face. "You actually think I killed someone, Detective?"

"It's just to eliminate you as a suspect," Jack answered deftly with copspeak. "Just a formality."

"A formality, sure," with a snicker, humoring the *jook-sing* cop now. He casually checked the calendar blotter on his desk. It didn't take a minute.

"I was at a Chinatown fund-raiser. At On Luck restaurant." He said it confidently, like he knew it would be verified. An airtight alibi. "Ask any of the managers."

"What if I tell you"—Jack leaned forward—"that Jun's death leads back to your house?" He watched as smooth James Gee *saang* slowly became Bossy Gee.

"My house?" Bossy looked puzzled. "Get to the point, Detective. What are you implying?"

"It may have to do with the home invasion you suffered recently."

Bossy leaned back, frowned toward the file cabinets. "I don't see any connection to that. And I don't like to talk about it. My family is still in mourning. And I explained everything to the New Jersey police already."

"I understand your grief," Jack said.

"I don't think you do," Bossy said. "My father died a horrible death, suffocating, and a heart attack."

"It's possible Jun gave your address to the home invaders," Jack continued.

Bossy shook his head, annoyed now, the *chaai lo* trying his patience. *Not so friendly anymore*, thought Jack.

"Where are you getting all this?" Bossy asked skeptically. "My family doesn't need any more bad news."

"It may have to do with a gambling debt," suggested Jack. Bossy took a breath, sighed. "Troubled employee, gambling debt, home invasion," he said dismissively. "Aren't you taking this a bit far, *Yu*?"

"Only as far as I need to, *sir*," Jack countered.

Bossy paused, his annoyance quickly switching to resignation. "What does your father do?" he finally asked.

"*Keuih jouh yee gwoon,*" Jack answered. "He was a laundryman."

Bossy cracked a smile that was almost a sneer, trying hard to mask his disdain for the American-born *son of a laundryman.* Jack didn't miss the contempt in his eyes.

"My father," Bossy said, glowing with arrogant pride, "was a hero in Chinatown. Ask *anyone.* A *great* man."

A great man, thought Jack sardonically, *who made dirty money off the vices that tugged at the souls of the lonely, isolated bachelors of Pa's generation. A "great" man, who was a* tong *member and Triad leader who trafficked in paper sons and concubine wives, and alcohol and opium.* Jack bit his tongue to keep the words from coming out.

"Isn't that even more reason to bring to justice those who cost him his life?" he asked instead.

"Look, suppose what you say is true," Bossy said. "Who do *you* think did it?"

"That's what I want to ask *you.* And I can't comment on an open investigation," Jack responded with more cop-speak.

"Of course not." Bossy smirked. "How convenient."

"How's that?" Jack narrowed his eyes.

"That you can make these *allegations,* without substantiating what your sources are."

"C'mon," Jack jabbed. "Who did it, Gee *saang?* Who do you think the perpetrators are?"

Bossy took a shallow breath through his nose. "I have *no* idea. That's what I told the New Jersey police."

"White, black, Asian?" Jack pressed.

"They wore ski masks and gloves. And it happened so fast I never got a good look. They all wore black sneakers or work boots. One of them had a shotgun."

"Your gut feeling?"

Bossy shrugged. "The Jersey police seemed like they thought it was a 'Chinese thing.' But they could be *gwai lo* devils for all I know. Maybe people who worked on the house. Deliverymen. It could be anyone."

"Why's that?"

"Someone said 'no fears' when they were beating me."

"'No fears'?"

"Right. In *English*."

"But why *your* house?"

"Who knows? There are people in this neighborhood who objected to me building this house. There are people who resent us for being successful."

"You mentioned that to the police?"

"They didn't want to hear it. I guess a 'Chinese thing' is more convenient."

"They just blurted out 'no fears'?"

"No. When they were pushing us around, I told them they were making a big mistake. They were binding my father at the other end of the living room."

"'A big mistake'?" *Arrogance even in the clutch of armed thugs?*

"I said it in English first. When I didn't get an answer, I repeated it in Chinese. Then one of them belted me a couple of times with his gun. That's when someone punched me and said, 'No fears.' I was down and bound before I knew it." He took another breath before continuing. "Since then, I've discovered there have been a number of home invasions in this county. Some of the victims were Asian. The only ones arrested were *gwai lo* whites—I guess they resented *tong yen* for having money." He checked his watch, a shiny gold Rolex, showing his impatience now.

"I have a meeting to get to, Detective," he said.

"If you know who did this, and you want to keep the police out of it so you can resolve matters yourself, it's a bad idea."

A sneer muscled onto Bossy's lips again. "I've cooperated fully with the police. I hope they do their job."

"And if Jun did get killed because he gave up your address," Jack continued, "and you *know* something about it and keep it from us, that could incriminate you as well."

"I've got nothing to hide."

Almost as if on cue, the receptionist's voice came over the phone speaker on his desk. "Your car is waiting downstairs now," she announced. Bossy stood up behind the desk, indicating the meeting was over.

Jack stood up as well. "Thanks for your time, Gee *saang*," Jack said coolly, heading for the door before turning back again. "Just one more thing. I'll need to speak to your son. Frank, is it?" He watched Bossy's face turn pink, then red.

"Why?" Bossy's eyes narrowed. "He wasn't there that night."

"Just routine." Jack smiled into Bossy's taut mask. "Just to eliminate him from the scenario."

"Well, he doesn't come home much. And he keeps changing his phone number." Bossy's eyes showing Jack to the door now.

The son trying to evade law enforcement? Jack dropped another NYPD detective's card on the desk.

"If you speak with him, please ask him to call me."

"Certainly," Bossy replied, but the look on his face said, *Like hell I will.*

Jack went out and nodded to the smiling receptionist as he left. When he got downstairs, the street was crowded with late-afternoon activity, but he didn't see Bossy's car waiting anywhere.

He decided not to wait for Franky Noodles's phone call and went up Pell to pay Half-Ass a visit.

When he passed Doyers Street, he noticed a red Camaro parked at the bend, halfway onto the sidewalk. *Bossy's kid must be in the vicinity.*

Half-Ass looked like its name: a half-ass paint job on a half-ass renovation of what was once a Chinatown association front. A Hip Ching *tong* storefront on the shortest street in Chinatown.

A simple hand-painted sign hung above the door and picture window. In big-brush block letters KONG SON RES-TAURANT, with a few smaller Chinese characters and the number 9, for 9 Pell Street. Kong Son was the official business name, but local *jook sings*—American-born Chinese, or ABCs—had nicknamed the place Half-Ass for its appearance. But their fast-food plates were notori-ously popular. It was a place frequented by locals and Pell Street regulars, with a big takeout trade to *tong* affiliates. It was a pit stop for Chinatown truckers and car-service jockeys breaking for a quick hit of China-town comfort food.

Pa had brought Jack here many times as a kid.

HE PUSHED IN through the squeaky aluminum door and ordered a cup of *jai fear* at one of the stools along the coffee counter, casually scanning the room as he waited. *The small front tables empty.* He glimpsed a customer stepping away from the hot-plates counter: *short*, maybe five-six but built thick like a *foo* dog under the tight designer leather jacket. Moving like he thought highly of who he was, carrying a generous plate of *gee pa faahn* back to his table of gangbangers. They were Black Dragons, easy to see by the dragon tattoos on their hands, arms, and necks.

Turning to the steamy wall mirror above the coffee and tea stations, Jack viewed the gang near the back wall. The round table had a group of eight: four young Chinese gangbangers, three of their groupie girlfriends, and, from the memory of a scowling cemetery photo in Jack's mind, one Francis "Franky Noodles" Gee. The Foo Dog.

The other gangsters tried to keep their backs to the wall.

The girls looked fourteen but were probably eighteen and wore a dozen tropical colors highlighted into their feathered hairstyles. The four wannabes wore spiky punk hair and leather jackets, looked more like players in a rock band than stone-cold fighters in a vicious street gang.

The girls nursed their bubble teas and giggled while the guys cussed, smoked cigarettes, and drank fluorescent-colored soda.

Franky, who looked noticeably older than the pack around him, was the only one chowing down this afternoon.

Jack's cup of *jai fear* arrived, and he spooned in some sugar without taking his eyes off Franky. It was clear to him that Franky wasn't Sing's killer. *Too short*, according to the ME's profile, and, as Jack could see watching him fork a piece of pork into his mouth, *not left-handed.*

Leaving a dollar on the counter for his coffee, Jack stepped to the Dragons' table, attracting wary looks from a few of them. When he pulled back a chair and sat, the table went silent.

Jack quietly laid his gold shield on the table and pulled back his jacket to reveal the butt of his Colt Special. Franky gave the groupie girls a look, and they left Half-Ass, *carrying*, Jack knew, the gang's guns in their knockoff designer handbags. It was common practice in Chinatown gangland; no one got busted for weapons possession, and any cop who pulled a gun would have to justify it.

Franky and Jack glared at each other, but both knew better, wisely choosing to play it cool and see what the deal was before they ruined Half-Ass's afternoon.

"So *what?*" Franky said, shrugging as Jack put his badge away.

"So I just met with your father," Jack said.

"That right?" Franky's nonchalant response drew sniggers from the four Dragon boys.

"Know what for, *Francis?*" Franky's frown indicated he didn't like the mocking way Jack used his name.

"You picked up your weekly *bribe?*" he countered. All the Dragons snickered.

"You really want to talk 'home invasion' in front of the scrubs?"

The snickering stopped.

"Better check the streets, boys," Franky said, "before your *dailo* gets pissed off again." They left Half-Ass as Franky went back to scarfing down his pork-chop rice. "I wasn't home that night," he said between bites.

"I know you have an alibi for that night," Jack offered.

"Yeah, and like I was going to rob my own family, *right*."
Franky shook his head.

"But if it's got anything to do with why a body floated
onto my desk," Jack said, "you'd better say something
now."

"I don't know anything about that." Smooth, like his
father, like he had experience being coached by counsel.

"Your B-team tuned up a Ghost named Doggie Boy and
got my victim's name."

"I don't know anything about *that*, either," Franky
repeated coolly.

"Then a couple of weeks later, my vic winds up dead."

"Again, *Detective*, I know nothing about this." Franky's
tone, *like father like son*, was superior. "But if what you say is
true, the Ghosts should be your main suspects."

"You like the Ghosts for the home invasion?"

"Sure. You say they had the information, they're good
for it. And those fuckers are the only ones with the balls to
pull it off."

But why would they kill Sing? wondered Jack. *Not like Jun
Singarette was going to talk about any of it.*

"That's not enough," Jack said.

"My father told you about one of them saying, 'No fears'?"

"He did."

"'No fears' is the slogan of some of the senior Ghost boys'
crews. They think they're hot shit."

"You told your father this?"

"What do *you* think?" Franky said.

"I think Ghosts hit your father's house," Jack said. "But I
don't think they whacked my victim."

"That right?" Sarcasm again.

"I think *you* guys got the real motivation," Jack said. "Like *payback*."

"Wasn't me," Franky said. "Wasn't us."

"Where were you four nights ago?" Jack pressed.

"Gambling, like every night." Franky sighed. "Then karaoke, in the basements."

"Going to be a *lot* of witnesses for that, I bet."

"Yeah, *right*."

"Give me a reason to believe *any* of that's true."

Franky finished his *gee pa*, pushed the plate aside. "Give me a reason why I should even continue talking to you."

"No, you give *me* a reason," Jack said, "why I shouldn't have Traffic Division ticket and tow that shiny red car of yours every time it's in Chinatown. Tell me why I shouldn't get your probation violated over hanging out with known criminals in a known organized-crime location. Tell me why your Chinese ass doesn't want to get sent back to Rahway or Trenton State, even for a minute."

Franky was taken aback by what Jack knew about him.

"I didn't *violate* nothing," he said meekly.

"You're violating my intelligence, *kai dai*, so let's stop fucking around," Jack said. "You all beat my vic's name out of your rivals, and he winds up dead."

Franky took a breath, licked his lips. "But I didn't *violate* nothing," he quietly insisted.

"Maybe I don't think *you* did it. But I know you know something about it."

"Okay." Franky surrendered an answer. "I would have done it, *gladly*, if Father hadn't shut us down. He never liked the gangs involved in our family business and forced us out of it."

"He was going to handle it?"

"I didn't say that," Franky said. "I'm just telling you that we didn't do it. Not me, not my boys."

"Your father kept you out of it?"

"Correct."

There was a silent moment as Jack fought back a smile. He'd let Franky Noodles off the hook for now but realized he had a new angle on Bossy Gee. *If father and son didn't do it, who did?*

On the street outside Half-Ass, he could see two Dragons peering into the storefronts, moving along.

The answers, Jack had a hunch, were *here*, on this street, in the Hip Ching gambling den behind Half-Ass, at Bossy's realty office, and in other locations in Bossy's underworld. But not *now*, Jack knew, not in daylight. He'd return after dark, he decided, when Chinatown nightlife controlled the streets.

He watched as Franky Noodles waved to the counterman on the way out, suddenly in a hurry to get back to his red Camaro.

Fish in a barrel, Jack mused as he exited Half-Ass.

HALF-ASS WAS A twenty-four-hour greasy spoon, home to Pell Street regulars and Chinatown truck drivers dropping in for a quick *yeen gnow* or *hom gnow faahn* meal deal.

After sunset, most Chinatown families were home for the evening, surrendering the day to family dinner, Hong Kong videotapes, Chinese TV variety shows.

Families cooked their own rice in an electric pot and prepared a wok full of hot stir-fried vegetables, later adding in fast-food sides of *sook sik cha siew* roast pork, *for yook, see yow gai*, soy-sauce chicken, from takeout joints like Half-Ass.

Later at night, the local denizens who frequented Half-Ass weren't so family oriented: Chinese gamblers from the basements, voracious johns from Fat Lily's or Chao's cathouses, *see gay* drivers, cabbies, Black Dragon gang kids, made members of the Hip Ching *tong*, and their cronies.

All the seedy, shady creatures of the night, *their* dirty playtime until dawn.

JACK RETURNED TO Chinatown at midnight, made his way to the corner of Mott and Pell. The area was deserted except for an occasional passerby and what looked like a few gang kids at the far end of the short street.

All the office windows in the corner building were dark, but he noticed the black bulk of a radio car parked outside 36 Pell. There was no driver in the *see gay*, which made Jack wonder if this could be Bossy's car. He pulled out a pen and jotted the license number on his wrist anyway.

Farther up the block he could see a few people outside Half-Ass, shuffling and stamping their feet against the cold. They'd probably been gambling in the basement that extended beneath Half-Ass and had come up for air, maybe a change of luck.

Jack knew to go through the doorway adjacent to Half-Ass, into the courtyard behind, and down the short flight of concrete steps to the basement. Sometimes the kitchen *da jop* gathered outside the back exit of Half-Ass, taking their smoke breaks in the courtyard, tempted themselves by the card games, the flow of gamblers, and the large sums of cash money exchanging hands under their feet.

Jack kept his head down. Half-Ass was half full, its windows foggy as he went past, through the grimy corridor into the cement courtyard.

He stepped down into the basement. He nodded and grunted at an old man seated on a metal folding chair near the door, and that seemed enough to let him slide into the mix. The basement was crowded, and he lit one of Billy's Marlboros before feigning interest behind one of the *chut jeung* card games while covertly scanning the room. The usual assortment of restaurant workers off the late shift and gang kids, other losers returning from Atlantic City or Foxwoods with their last-ditch bets.

Mostly men smoking up a cloud of cigarette haze, matching expletives in Toishanese and Cantonese across the half-dozen rectangular tables. Only traditional poker games here—*chut jeung, sup som jeun*—seven-card and thirteen-card poker. No *dew hei* pussy mah-jongg games here. Women played mah-jongg.

No Las Vegas–style nights here. No casino games, just a notorious Chinatown Chinese poker joint. The Ghosts were way ahead by comparison, much more innovative than the Hip Chings, offering blackjack and mini-baccarat for the ladies at their gambling joints.

Here on Pell Street, men bet a week's pay or more on the number of buttons in a *fan tan* bowl, on a color or a favorite table. *Now that's manly!* Legendary players have won restaurants, or lost them. Their houses, their cars, their passports, and Rolex watches.

The gambling basements swallowed everything.

At the rear of the floor, the gang kids who had any money left had pooled their dollars and were betting together, cussing as their collective *bao* slowly disappeared.

Jack didn't see anyone his own height, mostly five-eight and under. Excluding the gang kids, nobody looked very suspicious, just another gathering of hard-luck stories, damaged people, and lonely lives.

He dropped ten bucks on top of one of the bet boxes drawn on the brown butcher paper covering the *sup som jeung* table. He lost that promptly, the dealer sweeping his money off the table with a grin.

He went to another table and peeled off a couple of Lincolns. He hadn't noticed any obvious left-handers slapping down money or cards on any of the tables. Dropping a Lincoln onto one of the end boxes, he won ten bucks. *Pure luck.*

Occasionally he'd jerk his eyes up abruptly, flash scanning the tables to see if anyone was paying any particular attention to him. *No one seemed to care.*

Deciding to see if any *persons of interest* were up in Half-Ass, he headed back to the courtyard. He grunted toward the old man on the way out, who seemed pleased that he was leaving.

He crossed the cement courtyard, back into the grimy building corridor leading out to Pell, when the first blow came over his left shoulder. It struck him hard across the back of his head, sent him reeling forward into the wall of the narrow hall. Something *metal.*

The second and third blows came in rapid hits on his neck and shoulders as he threw up a blocking arm and fought for balance. A jackhammer knee drove him to the dirty linoleum floor.

He yelled and started to draw his Colt, his head spinning. Twisting away from the direction of the attack, he caught the flash of a man in dark clothes darting out to Pell Street.

He struggled to his feet, the Colt in hand now, trigger finger ready.

When he staggered out of the building the street was empty, the neon colors of the restaurant and bar signs swimming in his head. He took a few cold *shaolin* breaths, *stabilizing*, but it wasn't until a few minutes later, when he'd regained his equilibrium, that he realized the black *see gay* was no longer parked in front of 36 Pell.

The cold night air had revived him a bit, and he went directly to Grampa's, three blocks away.

In the blue darkness of one of the booths, the barmaid gave him half a bag of ice, which he used as cold compress to his head, shoulders, and neck. It was a warning, he knew. He'd been hit hard enough to stun but not to kill. Besides a few lumps, he couldn't find any blood on himself. If they'd wanted him dead, they'd have snuffed him.

The ice dulled the pain, and Grampa himself sent a boilermaker over to his solitary booth. Jack dropped the shot glass into the beer mug, chugged half of it back. He could feel the alcohol flowing to his brain and cooling down the pain inside him.

The warning only strengthened his resolve. He knew he had to be close to something if they'd felt the need to attack him. And they didn't care if he was a cop.

He threw back the rest of the boilermaker, pulled out his cell phone, and called for a radio car back to Sunset Park. First thing in the morning, he determined, he'd run the license-plate number he'd scrawled on his wrist on the DMV and the Traffic Division databases.

Night Rider 2

ONE IN THE morning and he was restless, his last night in the Edgewater house. He poured some XO into a tumbler, gulped a hit, and took his last look around the dark kitchen, the curtained living room.

It isn't the fifty thousand cash they've stolen, Bossy thought—he'd make that back in a month. Nor the three Rolex watches, which were payment swag from a Chinatown jewelry-store owner who'd gambled and lost down number 15 basement. He didn't care about all that, almost as if the money lost were something he'd kept handy, for ransom, for just the circumstances that occurred. *All part of the deadly circle of money,* he thought. *No big loss.*

But what did matter was his father's death. He could never forgive *that. The great Duck Hong dying like that, with a whimper.* He knew nothing would bring his father back, but the *face* of it was unforgivable. They'd stolen what amounted to *death money.*

The Hok Nam Moon Triad elders would also certainly retaliate for the death of a senior brother, especially against the On Yee and the Red Circle member Fay Lo. It was more than the Hip Chings could handle, but the Hok Triad could carry the fight from Hong Kong through its many members in the overseas cities and communities to wherever the On Yee had a presence. They'd already battled in Chinatowns in Boston, Montreal, Toronto, and San Francisco, but vengeance would be paid out over the seasons, measured but forceful and significant. Some of it was payback for feuds dating back a hundred years.

Bossy poured some more XO, tossed it back. *Just lay low*, he was told. *Don't draw attention to the Triad*.

This wasn't only a little turf battle between the earners on the street anymore. Of course, the fighting between the Dragons and Ghosts would continue until their *dailo* were replaced, but the Triad took over, advised Bossy to stay out of it. The less he knew, the better.

Bossy disagreed. "He's *my* father, *my* family. I deserve a say in it." With regard to the On Yees and Fay Lo, he'd deferred to the Hok Nam Moon: *let the Triads battle it out and wash the fat troublemaker*. He agreed to keep a low profile and was determined to keep his enthusiastic son Franky out of it. The idiot was an easy target—everyone knew he was Bossy's son—careless and reckless, wanting to descend into the pit of America as fast as his hero older brother, Gary, had wanted to ascend.

Let the street gangs do their work.

Let the Triad big boys do their work.

But regarding the matter of the takeout deliveryman who'd betrayed them, he'd wanted a *personal* touch, not some psycho hit man from Hong Kong intruding into his family affairs.

He preferred someone he could trust, someone who was familiar with the days and nights of his life. Someone who knew his family's background and had exhibited loyalty.

The Hok Nam Moon relented, and they'd quickly come to an agreement on who would begin the retributions.

No one was surprised, not even the killer.

But Bossy *was* surprised, though not shocked, at the *jook sing* Chinese cop showing up so quickly at his doorstep and office. He had hoped that the matter would have simply disappeared, washed away forever.

The *chaai lo* annoyed him more than unnerved him.

It had caused him to make a few phone calls.

He finished the XO as a white wash of car headlights swept across the kitchen walls. He lit a Marlboro and watched the walls dim and then fade to dark again. After a minute he could hear tires crunching gravel, then the purring engine of the black car outside. He checked his Rolex. *Right on time.* The headlights flashed off. He imagined the driver, Mon Gor, waiting patiently, but *always ready to go on a moment's notice.*

The XO and the nicotine leveled the tension, refocused him on more immediate, primal needs. He'd considered a quick trip to one of the strip clubs. The roomy black car always reminded him of the sex jaunts to Booty's, which had always provided a secluded spot for blow jobs from the dancers. Mon Gor knew the drill and always exited the car for a *cigarette* walk, far enough for a ten-minute BJ on the backseat.

Bossy rejected the thought of Fat Lily's; too many Chinatown johns knew him there, and the whores weren't as pretty. Instead he imagined himself at Chao's, on the edge of Chinatown, picking the youngest-looking *siu jeer* out of the lineup.

The alcohol rushed through his blood and made his balls tingle.

Finishing the cigarette, he tossed a last angry look toward the dark living room and headed for the waiting car.

Transporter 1

It was snowing lightly the next morning as Jack zipped back to Chinatown in a *see gay* out of Sunset Park.

The Chinese driver maintained a running dialogue with his radio dispatcher, injecting a few murmured expletives between the static lines.

Jack scanned the dark sky above the slick highway, shook his head. Of course, he didn't think Bossy himself stabbed Sing through the heart, hauled him through the freezing water, and shoved him off into the Harlem River. He didn't do the dirty work; he hired people for that. Contracted it out. Or the *tong* arranged it, and they were all complicit.

"Fuck your mother!" the driver hissed. "*Dew nei lo may,*" to his dispatcher. It broke Jack's focus as the driver swerved to exit off the BQE and back onto the streets.

"*Jong che,*" dispatch squawked. "Accident on the Brooklyn Bridge! Avoid!"

The driver turned the black car around toward the Manhattan Bridge, the next-nearest Chinatown crossing.

Jack noticed the driver's knowledge of the routes, figured it was part of the business of transporting people from one place to another destination. Those destinations could be airports, train and bus terminals, and the city had many other points of interest. But if you drove the overnight shift, it was a different clientele. Sure, the airports and terminals were still there, but so were the nightclubs, the gambling joints, the motels, and the whorehouses. All the all-night dives like Half-Ass and Grampa's and Lucy Jung's.

The interior of the car was gray, dark as the sky outside, but clean, without magazines or personal items, unlike the cars of some of the drivers who used their own family vehicles to make extra money.

Always on call, Jack thought, *real Chinese cowboys. Saddle up, ride out.* A lot of single or divorced men. The lifestyle didn't help family life. These were the men who disdained the obsequious restaurant work of their peers, the back-breaking labor of the Chinatown *coolie* construction gangs, the grinding days of the street vendors in the heat and freeze and rain and snow.

No, they preferred to mount their leased, air-conditioned Town Cars to ferry others to destinations sometimes deemed *illegal*, but where the tips were better than good and where one could do well in the *gwai lo* city.

There were no other clues in the *see gay* car. No family photographs or Chinese saints on the dashboard. No faux-Chinese firecrackers hanging off the rearview mirror. No takeout containers or water bottles or Chinese newspapers.

Just another hustling guy trying to make a few extra bucks.

But of course he didn't think Bossy himself did the killing. Franky Noodles, either: *Too obvious, and he doesn't fit the profile.* They'd kept him out of it, had protected the wannabe golden boy.

The radio car crossed the Manhattan Bridge before Jack knew it and was rolling into Chinatown. The driver drifted his car right, down through Fukienese East Broadway and around to Confucius Towers, a block's walk to the Fifth Precinct.

If it wasn't Bossy, it's someone he trusted.

He paid the driver an extra five and crossed Bowery from Confucius Towers toward the Fifth Precinct.

Run DMV

THE KNOTS AT the back of his head, neck, and shoulders grabbed at him, but Jack had spread on the *mon gum yow*,

Tiger Balm, let it do its mentholated relief work for him. The shift cops wrinkled up their noses as he passed. He went to the second floor of the Fifth Precinct, to the main computer, and logged in.

According to the Department of Motor Vehicles database, the black Lincoln Town Car was five years old, a 1990 model that was leased by and registered to Golden Mountain Realty. *Bossy's company.*

When he ran the plate numbers through the Traffic Division site, the connection became even clearer. Over the past two years, the Town Car had received four traffic violations: one for running a red light near Chinatown, issued to Francis Gee, Bossy's *bad seed*, aka Franky Noodles. The fine was paid by Golden Mountain Realty.

Two tickets were for daytime standing in a no standing zone. From the addresses on the tickets, Jack remembered the locations of the Lucky Dragon and China Village, two of Bossy's Bronx restaurants. The last violation was for an illegal U-turn in the South Bronx six months earlier, on a street not far from Booty's, or Chino's, strip club. Late at night.

Those three tickets were issued to driver Mak Mon Gaw and were paid off by Lucky Food Enterprises. *Another of Bossy's companies,* figured Jack. The NYS driver's license for Mak identified him as male, with brown eyes, his height five feet eleven inches. His photo face was the every face of a middle-aged Chinatown man. Black hair, dark eyes giving a Long March stare. An expressionless face, unremarkable, *inscrutable.* Waiter, accountant, laborer, entrepreneur, *everyman.* Nothing to indicate he was a cabbie or chauffeur or radio driver. His date of birth was February 2, 1951, which made him forty-four years old. *Forty-four,* mused Jack, *an unlucky Chinese number that sounds like "double-death" in Cantonese. Born in the Year of the Tiger.* Mak had a Chinatown address: 8 Pell Street, apartment 3A. *A Hip Ching apartment on a Hip Ching street,* Jack figured, *diagonally across from Half-Ass.*

He ran Mak Mon Gaw for priors or warrants, but the man had no criminal history. The way the name was romanized indicated he was from Hong Kong, or China, originally. Jack reconsidered him as a *person of interest* and was about to access the Immigration Department's database when his cell phone buzzed.

The female dispatcher's voice asked, "What's your *twenty,* Detective Yu?"

"Fifth Precinct," he answered. "Computer room."

"Stand by," she instructed.

He was puzzled by the call, proceeded to print out the information he'd accessed. He was folding the copies into his pocket when footsteps thumped up to the second floor, coming in his direction.

Two hulky shadows appeared in the doorway. Their faces looked familiar, and no introductions were necessary. *Internal Affairs.* Hogan and DiMizzio, big white cops with neat haircuts and eyes like steel rivets. They'd investigated Jack previously, after the murder of Uncle Four in Chinatown.

Jack had been wondering *when* it would come, the IA inquiries, popping open the case like a poison pus pimple, with their innuendoes, their boldfaced lies, the tough-cop-and-honest-cop routines. It hadn't taken long this time, less than two days after he'd picked up Bossy's trail. A day after interviewing him in his office.

It was clear Bossy was sending a message, saying *who he was* by siccing the IA cops on him.

They stepped into the room with the same contemptuous attitudes on their faces.

But it didn't surprise Jack this time, and the pressure only confirmed that he was pushing in the right direction.

Hogan kicked it off. "Up to old tricks, huh, Yu? *Harassment?*"

"Setting up a *shakedown*, huh?" DiMizzio taunted. Jack shook his head, didn't dignify the insults with a response.

"Detective Yu," Hogan said, "can you explain why you were in the South Bronx on Thursday night, February fifteenth?"

"Where you encountered a plainclothes detail from the Four-One?" DiMizzio said.

It was the same quick questioning, eye-swiveling routine, meant to keep the subject off balance. It didn't faze Jack this time.

"I was *off duty*," Jack said. "Me and a friend went for a drive. We took the east side, the FDR, to the Bronx. We were crossing over for the West Side Highway back to Manhattan when we ran into the plainclothes guys."

The answer seemed to satisfy them; if they'd had more, they'd play it out. But Jack knew they were working him, just warming up.

"Why did you interview James Gee?" asked Hogan.

"Normal course of investigation," answered Jack. "Just due diligence."

"And questioning his son?" asked DiMizzio.

"The guy had priors." Jack shrugged. "He was a natural suspect."

"Enough for you to visit his house in New Jersey?"

"Normal course of investigation," repeated Jack.

"So what led you to Mr. Gee's doorstep?" Hogan asked.

Jack gave them an abbreviated account of his investigation. He couldn't tell them about Ah Por's yellow witchcraft, the assistance from his incipient alcoholic Chinatown pal Billy Bow, nor about the illegal Chinese gambling and drug-dealing places he'd visited or the criminal element he'd been around.

"That's *it?*" DiMizzio cracked.

"So," Hogan added, "you're going by the words of disgruntled co-workers, illegal wetbacks, some gossip from old men, and the convenient bullshit from an ex-con Chinatown gangbanger trying to save his own ass?"

"Yeah, if that's how you want to put it," Jack said with a mock grin.

"Mr. Gee gives you an alibi," DiMizzio said with a frown, "but you choose to ignore that."

"The man practically offered me a bribe," Jack said, "a security job. Is that what he promised you for dogging me off the case?"

"You got something against rich people?" DiMizzio asked.

"*You* wouldn't. That's because you get off on catching cops, not criminals."

"What's with the smart mouth, Yu?" snapped Hogan.

"Just taking a page from IA," Jack said. "It fits the *tone* of your question, right?"

"Yeah, well, we'll be watching you, *smart ass,*" said DiMizzio.

"Look," Hogan said, "just stay the fuck away from James Gee, got it?"

Jack bit his tongue and cursed silently as the two IA bulls turned and stomped out. He waited until their footsteps receded before following the trail back to Pell Street.

Golden City

BOSSY WATCHED FROM the backseat of the Town Car as Mon Gor loaded a case of Remy from the Golden City basement into the trunk. Bossy hadn't told Mon Gor about the visit from the Chinese cop. What the Triad had advised him held true for Mon Gor also: *the less he knew, the better.* The *chaai lo* would drop the case soon anyway, he thought. Bossy leaned back and recollected what he knew about his longtime driver, who'd driven him to and from all the places of his overnight debauchery: whorehouses like Chao's, Fat Lily's, and Booty's, where he liked his young, dark-skinned *see yow gay*, soy sauce pussy.

Mon Gor was rangy, almost as tall as Bossy himself. He'd arrived in Chinatown in the 1970s and, as an accommodation to the Hok Nam Moon Triad, Duck Hong hired him as a truck driver for the noodle company. He was around twenty years old then, around forty now.

All the trips to the racetracks—Aqueduct, Belmont, Roosevelt, and Yonkers.

All the bars and clubs, like Lucy Jung's, Grampa's, Yooks, Wisemen, Macao, China Chalet, or the Chinese Quarter. All driven to by Mon Gor.

All the hot sheets joints and happy-ending massage parlors on the outskirts of Chinatown.

His father, Duck Hong, had told Bossy that Mon Gor was once one of the top kung fu students in Hong Kong, a *wing chun* man. There were stories about his heroics in Chinatown bar brawls. Soon after, he became Duck Hong's personal driver, also reluctantly driving the Gee women to facials and massages, to mah-jongg games and *yum cha*. Driving his son Francis *wherever* until he happily got his own license at the age of seventeen.

Now the women were gone, and so was his father. And Francis had his own car, the obnoxious red one.

Now it was just him and Mon Gor. Bossy and driver.

Mon Gor headed back to the kitchen entrance for another box. Provisions for the condo Bossy'd agreed to try out, on the edge of Sunset Park. A two-week *free trial* run, fully furnished. The two weeks allowed him to scout the rest of waterfront Brooklyn, near the East River bridges. Extra time to consider other condominium developments, funded by Triad money behind barely legit front corporations.

He was relieved not to go back to Edgewater. And happy to be so close to Manhattan.

Mon Gor waited by the doorway for one of the *da jop* from the kitchen. His friends and associates had twisted his name Mak Mon Gaw into *Mon Gor*, a nickname, which in Cantonese sounded like "night brother."

Because he usually worked at night, driving the denizens of the dark hours.

Nobody ever saw him in daylight, except Bossy and occasionally the family. It was like he was invisible in daylight, this barroom avenger, who was rumored to be a Triad man himself. He'd supposedly intervened in three near fights in the Hip Ching gambling basements, resulting beneficially to the Pell Street *tong*.

But in daylight he was invisible.

* * *

MON GOR TOOK a box from the puzzled kitchen worker and came back to the car trunk. A big box of roast duck and *for yook* and *see yow gay*. *Fast food* snacks would suffice until he had a chance to check out the takeout counters in Sunset Park Chinatown. Bossy straightened as Mon Gor slammed the trunk shut.

"*Gau dim*," Mon Gor said in his slang Cantonese, "all done." It was the same answer he'd given the Triad elders when asked if he'd *washed* the first matter, of the traitorous deliveryman. *All done*.

Snow flurries began falling from the slate Bronx sky.

"*Gau dim*," Mon Gor repeated almost to himself as he slid behind the wheel and glanced at the rearview mirror.

"Good," Bossy said. "Now drop me off in Brooklyn and you're done."

"*Mo mun tay*, Bossee," Mon Gor answered. "No problem." He fired up the engine and pulled the car away from the curb, turning for the FDR drive south.

Sunset Park and then home to Pell Street.

Mo mun tay at all.

Mak the Knife

THE SNOWFLAKES GOT thick and heavy, and Jack left a trail of dark footprints in the thin layer of white that covered the way back to Pell Street.

Number 8 Pell, Mak Mon Gaw's address, was an old four-story, redbrick building that dominated the north corner of Pell and Bowery. The storefronts along Pell included a Chinatown gift shop, a China travel agency, and a Buddhist temple, but on the Bowery side the building was anchored by Bamboo Garden restaurant, a Chinese grocery store, and a small bakery.

In big block letters, the word ORIENTAL was still visible, high up on the faded green façade that overlooked the boulevard.

Jack noticed there were two sets of fire escapes on the Pell Street side, but just one set above the Bowery side, which led him to believe the main exit for the building's tenants was number 8.

He went through the unlocked street door, a bad habit from an earlier time when Chinatown people didn't bother to lock their front doors, when crime was almost nonexistent.

Times had changed.

Jack looked at the mailboxes. Unlike some of the older Chinatown tenements where the tenants all had their own scattering of mismatched metal boxes screwed into the wall, number 8 Pell had an old but standard split panel of metal mailboxes, recessed into the wall. The mail carrier keyed open the top panel, folded it down, and inserted the mail. Then he relocked it.

Each individual mailbox was vented so the tenants could see if they'd had mail delivered. There were three vertical rows of six mailboxes each, meaning there were eighteen apartments in the building.

These mailboxes meant that the building had been renovated over the decades and now had more new families than the old flow of transient single men. A few of the tenants' names had been neatly typed and inserted into the little slot at the top of each mailbox. *Newer tenants*, figured Jack.

Some of the tags had been whited-out, with the new tenant's name in black marker staking a claim over it. *A newcomer tagging over another immigrant's story.*

Most of the mailbox name tags were old, meaning the tenants had lived here a long time, over generations of the same family, the apartment passed down. The name Jack was looking for, Mak Mon Gaw, was one of the old ones. It was just a crude lettering, MAK/GAW, that barely fit into the name slot.

MAK/GAW handwritten on yellowed paper, not touched in twenty years.

There wasn't any mail in his box.

Jack looked down at the baseboards, the floor, any tiles that might seem loose. He scanned the areas around both door frames, ran his fingers along the edges. He didn't find the spare key that top-floor tenants sometimes secreted downstairs just in case they got locked out. *Men*, whipped at having to call *lo por*, and having their wifeys come down four flights to chide them before letting them back into the building.

It didn't matter to Jack.

Chinatown was smaller then, he remembered, and he and his teenage pals had explored all the Chinatown rooftops, traveling across the heights the way immigrants did in the previous century. *Across the rooftops.* The rooftops ran evenly on both sides of the street until halfway down the block, near Doyer, where they butted up against taller buildings on the Bloody Angle. Still, someone could run across the rooftops on Pell and descend, emerging on Bayard or Bowery or Doyers or Mott. It was how the Hip Chings had defended their turf so well through the decades.

But only the people *who had to* went up and down.

Jack knew the rooftops here and how the apartments were situated. Mostly straight railroad flats and a mix of L-shaped, one-bedroom setups. People who *really had money* combined two apartments into one and occupied the entire floor.

Rent control ruled, but *fong day*, or key money, a *codicil*, gave landlords a cash trump card.

Along the way, Chinatown learned to play by its own insular set of rules.

THE STREET WAS a fresh layer of white. *See gay* drivers would keep their cars indoors during off-hours, saving themselves the trouble of scraping off eight inches of snow and ice before the next job, especially if they were working a wedding or driving out to a freezing Chinese burial at one of the cemeteries in Brooklyn or Queens.

There were only two indoor commercial parking garages in Chinatown. One was Municipal Parking, which was five blocks away on Pearl Street. A lot of local folks parked there. The other was more expensive, the Rickshaw Garage, which was just around the corner, a block and a half from Pell.

Jack decided to try Rickshaw first. *Keep the car close to home. Always good to go, ready to roll.*

AT RICKSHAW, JACK badged the garage manager, telling him a lie about investigating a stolen-car ring and requesting a list of long-term customers. He didn't want his real inquiries leaking out in case an attendant had a cozy relationship with a driver.

The manager called up the annual accounts listing on the

computer screen and showed Jack where to scroll the file. Jack quickly found the plate numbers he was hoping to find, numbers belonging to Mak Mon Gaw's Lincoln Town Car.

"Can you check the key log and tell me which of these vehicles is presently in the garage?" Jack asked.

"Most of our long-term customers use their cars to get to work," the manager offered. "*Early birds*, out at seven in the morning, back by seven at night." He took a quick key inventory, checked off the garaged cars for Jack.

The Town Car was still out.

"Seven to seven, huh?" Jack said. "I'll be back later."

HE CONSIDERED RETURNING to the Fifth Precinct but didn't want anyone reporting his ongoing investigation back to Internal Affairs. He also realized he hadn't eaten since before getting whacked across the head the night before and decided to buy takeout before dropping by the Tofu King.

Billy was busy managing the afternoon tofu rush, but offered Jack the use of his quiet little office at the back of the shop, where he could enjoy his *gnow nom faahn* in peace while trying to figure things out.

Jack wolfed down pieces of savory brisket and wondered about Bossy's driver. *Sure, it would have been easy to slip the lobby door lock of number 8 Pell, go up to 3A and cop-rap on the apartment door.* But banging on doors didn't always work in Chinatown, not if people were illegal immigrants or didn't respect the police, especially *yellow* police. He didn't want his *person of interest* to get nervous, maybe disappear, before he could question him.

The man had worked for Bossy Gee for years. Maybe the

family trusted him. *Dependable, steady.* Maybe he had some insight into the home invasion, about Bossy's intentions, or about the Gee family indiscretions.

Based on the locations of his traffic violations, Mak Gaw was probably familiar with the Bronx, especially the South Bronx during an overnight illegal U-turn halfway between Booty's and the possible crime scene at the riverside pocket park in Highbridge. *He knows the area after dark.*

Jack reviewed the copy of Gaw's license. At five foot eleven inches tall, he fit part of the medical examiner's profile of the knife-wielding perp.

Jack finished off the brisket with the rice, measuring the distance from *person of interest* to *suspect.* He considered the dark angles of Gaw's surname.

Gaw sounded the same as *gow,* or *gao,* or *gau,* depending on the dialect and intent of reference. Based on the tone and accent, *gaw* meant "enough already," "to rescue," "a man's penis" (*luk gow*), "to teach," "a dog," and "old style."

The phonetics danced in Jack's mind, *teaching a dog in the old style.* A lesson in payback?

The other part of his name, Mak, as in *lo mok,* was the Cantonese equivalent of "nigger."

Having lived as a single man in Chinatown, Jack had found it convenient to buy takeout food regularly. Most single men didn't cook and got by on a wide variety of Chinese takeout.

Sooner or later, Gaw will have to come out for food. If he parked during the afternoon, he'd surface around evening. If Gaw returned to the garage late, it'd probably be better to sit on number 8 and wait, Jack figured.

He passed Billy loading buckets of tofu and decided to check Rickshaw Garage again.

"You ONLY LEFT a couple of hours ago," the manager said. He seemed annoyed as he checked the key log again. "It's still early. Most of the long-term haven't come back yet."

Jack could see that Gaw's Town Car was still out. "I'll be back," he repeated.

Outside, the snow had stopped falling, and the afternoon looked like evening. It occurred to him that if for some reason Gaw had parked the car elsewhere, he could very well be in the apartment already.

He left the garage through the Elizabeth Alley exit and went toward the Fifth Precinct down the street. He walked halfway down the block before he saw the undercover Impala he was looking for, the one he'd driven to Fort Lee the day before.

THE SERGEANT AT the duty desk looked like he was happy to be out of the cold. He said, "That old Chevy's headed for the mechanic's. Something hinky with the transmission, won't go over twenty. Can't catch *anyone* going twenty." He paused. "And the heater don't work."

"That's okay, Sarge," Jack said. "I'm not chasing anyone. And I'm not going far." *Just four blocks and parked on a stakeout.*

The sergeant raised his eyebrows, frowned, and blinked before tossing Jack the Impala's keys. "Knock yerself out, Detective," he said.

"Thanks, Sarge," Jack said fraternally, stepping his way out of the Fifth.

* * *

JACK FIRED UP the Impala, let it idle a few minutes before he geared it. The Chevy sputtered away from the curb, and he made a right on Canal, another onto Bowery. *Two blocks.* He took a slow right onto Pell, saw the street was sparsely trafficked, saw a few customers in Half-Ass as he rolled by. He continued past Doyers, pulled the junker halfway onto the sidewalk down from Macao Bar, and killed the engine.

He adjusted the rearview and the driver's-side mirrors to frame the street, number 8, and Half-Ass. Knowing it could turn out to be a long night's stakeout, he took a few *shaolin* breaths and leaned back. He watched the street through the side view.

He knew it would be wise to proceed with caution, remembering getting slugged in the head and knowing that Singarette had been killed by a single knife thrust.

The perp's got some fighting skills. His gun hand drifted instinctively to the Colt, brushed its solid metal bulk. *But I also got .38-caliber kung fu.*

The frigid temperatures had kept many people off the streets. Most of the people who came through Pell were taking a shortcut across to Mott, trying to get home. Some were stragglers who drifted to Macao Bar for drinks or to Half-Ass for diner fast foods.

He finished off the cooled container of *jai fear* and focused on the street. The other businesses were still open despite how deserted the street looked. Shifting to the rearview mirror, he imagined the faces of all the people who'd helped bring his case back to Chinatown: Sing's co-workers; the *tres amigos*, Luis, Ruben, and Miguel; Huong the

Vietnamese lady in red; lowlifes like Doggie Boy; with inad-
vertent clues from Bossy Gee himself and from his son
Francis "Franky Noodles." And without Billy Bow's timely
help, Vincent Chin's research, and even Ah Por's arcane
clues, he'd be at a loss on how to proceed.

He left the car to check for lights on in the top windows
of number 8. Two of the windows were lit by fluorescent
rings on the ceiling. He couldn't be sure which was apartment 3A and went back to the Impala.

Two hours had passed before he knew it. Only four people
went into number 8 Pell: a grandmother with a grade-school
child, a young woman with an infant. No one went in or out
of the travel agency or the gift shops.

Flight to Fight

ANOTHER UNEVENTFUL HALF hour went by.

In the rearview, a man turned the corner from Bowery
onto Pell, crossed over to Half-Ass, and went inside. Jack
rolled down the driver's-side window to get a better look.

The man came back out.

Tall enough, thought Jack, preparing to exit the Impala. In
the mirror he could see the man pull out a pack of cigarettes,
shake one out. He lit it and took a deep drag, held it until he
hissed out a slow stream of smoke and steam that hung in the
frozen air. Apparently waiting for his takeout, he glanced up
at the top floors of number 8.

Jack turned and watched him through the rear window as
he took another pull off the cigarette. The realization hit
Jack like a slap in the face, *He'd lit the cigarette with a lighter*

in his left hand. The mirrors had thrown Jack off. The man now held the cigarette in his left hand. *And he now fits the medical examiner's profile of the killer.*

Jack slid out of the Chevy, quietly closing the driver's door. He walked slowly toward Half-Ass thinking, *Brace him quick, watch his hands, and keep at arm's reach.*

The man looked back into Half-Ass like he was checking on his takeout. Jack started crossing over and saw that the man quickly took notice of him. *A look of recognition?* As Jack got closer, the man started to back away toward Half-Ass, toward the building hallway where Jack had gotten slugged. *He resembled the driver's license photo of Mak Mon Gaw.*

Jack didn't want him running into the gambling basement and immediately flapped open his jacket, flashing his badge.

"Hey *dailo!*" Jack called. "What's the rush, brother?" The man didn't answer, continued to back into the building entrance.

Jack reached for the man's shoulder only to have his hand deftly brushed aside, the man oddly smiling as he turned and dashed into the building. To Jack's surprise, he didn't head to the courtyard for the gambling basement but instead sprinted up the first flight of stairs leading to the upper floors. Jack sprinted after him, almost one flight behind. He braced himself with both hands as he dashed through the narrow landing, toward the next flight of uneven wood steps.

Two huffing flights up the stairway, Jack could see the man's heels, their footsteps thundering up the rickety stairs. His heart hammering as he continued the chase up.

He can escape to Doyers or Bowery, using the roof stairs or fire escapes going down.

The man made it to the roof door, charged through it with a grunt. The door swung back, slamming. Jack paused when he got to it, took quick warrior breaths, and drew the Colt.

He lowered his shoulder at the door, thinking, *He couldn't have gotten more than a few yards out.*

He barged onto the roof in a combat stance, sweeping a 360-degree arc with the Colt, wary of anything behind him.

The roof door slammed shut again, blocking out the dim light that came from the stairwell.

There was nothing but the darkness.

Two stories above the streetlamps. A cloudless sky, the only light from the full moon above. In the distance, condo lights from high-up picture windows of Confucius Towers, winking down at the Chinatown rooftops.

It was dead quiet except for the blood beating in his ears. *Doyers to his right. Bowery to his left. He has to be around here somewhere.* In his crouching advance, Jack scanned the inky roofscape as his eyes adjusted to the dark. A tangle of TV antennas, black, blocky skylights and stairwell sheds, rows of restaurant exhaust ducts, boiler-room chimneys, and scattered piles of construction debris everywhere.

Every step he took was black pitch beneath broken sheets of ice and snow. Everything looked like menacing shadows. There were too many places to hide, to duck behind. Chinatown rooftops were a good place to ambush a vic. Dark, isolated, quiet. No civilians to witness the crime.

He hadn't called it in, wasn't expecting backup cops. But

he knew he didn't want to end his career on a frozen China-town rooftop.

Ahead of him was the front roof edge, forty feet above Pell. He could see faint illumination from the streetlamps below.

Low walls that separated the rooftops ran on either side of him.

He took a few stealthy steps forward, changed his position, did another 360 sweep with the gun. *Look for the fire-escape landings.*

He heard a *thud* to his left, like something got knocked over. He found his balance and leaned in that direction. *Footsteps would have given more,* he thought. *But if someone tossed something as a decoy, a misdirection . . .*

He stepped to his left, glanced again over his shoulder as he moved forward. He caught a glimpse of something metallic in the moonlight and instinctively threw up a bow arm block. He felt the sting of cold steel as it sliced through his sleeve and bit into the bone of his elbow.

He fell backward onto the ice, his elbow taking the brunt of it. The swing of his gun hand smacked the Colt against a frozen hump and sent it clattering across the icy blackness. He could feel the blood gushing out of his arm and kicked upward at the attacking shadow, scuttling on his back, backward toward his Colt.

The attacker slashed at his legs, following with a series of lightning hoof kicks and dragon stamps, trying to stomp Jack off the roof, into oblivion. Sending heel kicks at his groin. The kicks came so fast and furious it felt like Jack was fending off *two* attackers.

Jack countered with a series of upward kicks and knee blocks, absorbing the attack with his legs. He looked back for the Colt, saw it gleaming on the snowy ice a body's length away.

The man tried a few squatting stabs that Jack blocked with his hands. The knife caught the flap of Jack's jacket and ripped it open. Still on his back, Jack continued to kick upward with leg blocks, trying to take out the attacker's knees. He forced his body backward, desperately trying to reach the gun.

He could see the knife in the moonlight, held high in the man's left hand. As he dove for the gun, the man leaped over him, positioning himself to bring the knife down.

Rolling over as he palmed the Colt, Jack squeezed off a blind shot over his shoulder. The blast froze the man as Jack straightened, jamming off another wild round as he rose on one knee.

The knife trembled in the man's hand.

Jack leveled the Colt on him and cocked the hammer. "Drop the knife!" he yelled. "*Drop it* or join your ancestors!"

The man waggled the knife. He had a long face with a clenched jaw, and his eyes looked demonic in the moonlight.

Jack blasted a round into the icy patch of roof between the man's legs, splattering snow over his feet.

"You feelin' me, *kai dai*?" Jack said with a snarl. He could feel the blood oozing down his left arm, warm and slick-sticky now. He cocked the hammer again.

The man wavered for another second, thought better of it, and finally dropped the knife.

"On your knees!" Jack ordered. "On the ground!"

The man slowly complied. Jack pushed a foot into his back and forced him prone, held the Colt on his neck as he cuffed him with his blood-wet hand. He reached over for the man's knife and dropped it into his jacket pocket.

Jack yanked him back up by the elbows and marched him back down the creaky stairs. He perp-walked him up Bowery, toward the station house. Running on adrenaline now, he hoped he wouldn't bleed out on the short two-block march to Elizabeth Alley.

"Gaw, right?" Jack challenged. "You slugged me the other night, didn't you?"

The man spat at the sidewalk, but his eyes were scanning the street as he stumbled along. He swiveled his head to check behind him, and Jack grabbed him by the collar.

"You're good when your target's not expecting it, huh?" Jack said, pushing him along. The man never responded, kept a frozen frown on his face as they turned from Bayard onto Elizabeth Alley, to the Fifth Precinct.

"You killed Zhang with a single stab because he wasn't expecting it. You coward bastard." Jack marched him past the duty desk and shoved him into the holding cage. He now belonged to the desk sergeant.

While the sergeant processed him, Jack carefully placed the bloody knife in a plastic baggie. He gave it to the sergeant, along with the DMV copy of Gaw's driver's license.

EMS arrived and tended to Jack's wounds, trundling him into an ambulance as they rolled him back to Downtown Medical. Jack knew they'd stitch him up, give him a few shots to kill the pain. He wanted to pass out but knew he couldn't, not before getting Gaw's prints and making a few phone calls.

He took a deep, fortifying breath, resisted the urge to close his eyes.

* * *

IT TOOK AN hour and a half to clean and sew him up and spike him, considered fast service and only because he was a cop. The twenty-two stitches on his left elbow and forearm, the bandaged shallower cuts on both knees and shins. He knew that by then Gaw would have been transferred to the Tombs, in detention and awaiting orders to be taken to Rikers.

He checked in on Lucky, still in a coma in the Critical Care ward at the other end of the building. His boyhood pal, Tat "Lucky" Louie, with IV tubes in his arms, a plastic respirator over his mouth. *Lucky*, wounded in a bloody shoot out that left most of his crew dead. Lucky, the sole survivor.

In the quiet room, he watched the slow rise and fall of Lucky's chest, listening for the soft *ping* of the machine that kept him alive. *That's it, brother? This is how it ends for you? Another gangbanger bites the dust?*

HE CAUGHT A ride with an EMS tech headed back to Chinatown on the evening meal run.

At the Fifth, the sarge handed Jack a copy of Gaw's prints.

"He wanted a phone call," the sarge said. "Had this lawyer's card in his wallet." The business card belonged to Solomon Schwartz. "But you know," Sarge said with a grin, "the shoddy service around here, the phones ain't working."

"Thanks, Sarge." Jack laughed weakly, heading back out to Bayard.

AT THE TOMBS, Jack asked the familiar officers for help.

"Anyone tries to bail him, *lose* the paperwork for a few

hours. I'll be back in the morning. This guy's in deep, and we don't want to *chase* him. *Trust* me. It'll be good press, and I'll make sure you won't regret it."

The Tombs officers allowed Jack to make phone calls, send fingerprint faxes and voice mail. When he finished, he took a cab to Sunset Park.

Back in his Brooklyn apartment, he stripped down carefully, avoiding the stitches. He remembered to set his clock alarm before exhaustion and the pain medication dropped him into oblivion.

Knowledge Is Power

IN DAYLIGHT, THE stitches looked uglier than the night before, and surface pain from the cuts on his legs pinched with every step.

He was still groggy when he arrived at the Tombs, the place already abuzz with the processing of the morning's criminals. He badged his way to the clerk's office in the back and found the faxes he was hoping for.

The first one was from the Royal Hong Kong Police Force, February 21, 1995:

> *RHKPF Headquarters Mongkok Station, Kowloon*
>
> *PRINT Subject Wanted in HK for triple homicide in 1975.*
>
> *DETAIN Subject indefinitely. Fax from*

> *Immigration and Naturalization Service to*
> *follow.*

In small type at the bottom of the fax:

> *Thanks, Inspector Chow Yin Fat RHKPF*

The second fax was more recent, from Interpol, short-hand for the International Criminal Police Organization.

> *PRINT Subject is Red Notice, wanted member*
> *of illegal Triad society, Hok Nam Moon.*
> *Absconded via Hong Kong 1975. Detain*
> *without fail. Immigration/Deportation to follow.*

A Red Notice was Interpol's highest level of alert, an arrest warrant that circulated worldwide.

If Gaw was a Triad true believer, he wasn't going to flip on Bossy or the Triad or whoever put him up to Sing's murder. *Maybe he'll take his chances with deportation.*

As Jack was pondering it, another fax chugged through the machine. It was a reply to Jack from the New York City Bureau of Records, referring to Gaw's Social Security number that he'd used on a license/DOT vehicle registration form. Following Jack's inquiry, the holder of that assigned Social Security number was declared inactive, dead in 1974.

A hunch has paid off.

Somehow, Gaw had managed to assume another Chinese identity, a dead man. Whether the Triad or Duck Hong's people had arranged the paper deal, Jack couldn't know, but he realized now that Gaw had been hiding in plain sight for two decades.

And he probably wasn't going to be cooperative.

JACK CROSSED OVER to the detention/holding side of the Tombs facility. There was a room with a small table where they brought Gaw to be interviewed.

"I know Gaw's not your real name," Jack started in street Cantonese.

Mak Mon Gor laughed quietly.

"I know you suckered Zhang with a bullshit abalone deal, then killed him," Jack said. "But I think someone put you up to it. It was your boss, Jook Mun Gee, wasn't it?"

"*Dew nei louh mou*," Gaw cursed. "Fuck your mother."

"I should have figured it earlier," Jack said.

"I should have killed you earlier," Gaw spat.

"What did Bossy offer you?" Jack challenged. "Money?"

"*Dew nei louh mou.*"

"You killed him in that little park."

"*Fock* you, mathafocker."

The door swung open, and an older man in a business suit entered the room. Gray hair, fiftyish. The man parked his expensive briefcase on the table.

"Interview's over," the man said. "I'm his lawyer." He slid his business card onto the table. "Solomon Schwartz."

Jack wasn't surprised, knew *legal* would appear sooner or later. "The interview was over *before* you got here," said Jack.

"It's an outrage, Detective," Schwartz complained, "not allowing a phone call from the precinct? He's been denied due process."

"The process isn't perfect," Jack said. "But I'll tell you

what's *due*, Counselor. A judge is going to remand without bail. Your 'motherfucker' client here is a flight risk. Not only did he try to kill a cop, but he's wanted for even more trouble than your fancy words can get him out of."

Gaw frowned and mumbled curses under his breath.

"I'll have him out in twenty-four hours," said Schwartz.

"I don't think so. Hong Kong's got first dibs. Interpol's tagged a Red Card on him, and Immigration's been notified."

Solomon just shook his head, uncertain if it was a bluff or if he'd been outplayed on the overnight by the Chinese detective.

"Here or at Rikers, it doesn't really matter," continued Jack. "I don't think he'll be staying long."

"How's that?" Solomon asked.

"Interview's over," Jack said with a smile. "Send Bossy my regards." He left the room throwing a last look in Gaw's direction. Gaw was still scowling, staying inside himself. *Could he have another card to play?* wondered Jack.

He left the Tombs, went past the guard booth. One of the overnight officers apologized. "Sorry about the lawyer," he said. "Prisoner claimed he was sick, needed medication. Needed to call his doctor. So they let him make a call. He spoke Chinese with someone."

"No problem," said Jack, figuring, *Gaw probably called Bossy, who called Schwartz.*

WITH CAPTAIN MARINO's help from the Fifth Precinct, Jack obtained two warrants—one for Gaw's Town Car, the other for his Pell Street apartment. Jack *borrowed* Gaw's keys from Property, headed for Rickshaw Garage first.

The manager recognized Jack and escorted him to the

Lincoln. The five-year-old car still looked in mint condition. According to the ticket, the car was returned a few minutes before Jack first spotted Gaw walking into Pell Street. But *where* he'd been prior didn't seem to matter much anymore. Jack waited until the manager left before sliding into the passenger side.

The interior of the car was pristine, a somber gray color, the same as the hundreds of other cars that the *see gays* drove to cemeteries, weddings, and proms. There was a box of tissues on the backseat. He checked under the seats, along the door panels, in the center console. *All clear.*

In the glove compartment he found some Hong Kong pop music tapes, a few transportation maps of the tri-state area, and tour brochures of Boston and Philadelphia Chinatowns. There were booklets from a car dealership, a pen from China Village restaurant, some auto wipes, and a plastic Ziploc bag with *wah moy, chan pei moy,* and hawthorn flakes, Chinese candies for the road. Otherwise, *all clear.*

He moved to the rear of the car and popped the trunk using Gaw's key. There was a plastic milk crate that served as a road emergency kit: flares, jumper cables, flashlight, tow rope, a can of tire inflator. To one side a roll of paper towels; some plastic takeout bags; a *gai mo so,* feather duster; and a can of air freshener. A collapsible shovel, an ice scraper-brush-combination tool. A carton of cigarettes, Marlboros, with a few packs missing. And no New York State tax stamp.

He placed the carton of cigarettes carefully into one of the plastic bags before checking the spare-tire storage well. Finding nothing there, he closed the trunk, taking only the smokes.

He left Rickshaw and walked the block and a half to

number 8 Pell. Slipping on the disposable latex gloves from the precinct, he keyed the street door, went up to the third floor. At apartment 3A he inserted the other key, twisted it, and entered. There was a wall switch just inside the door, and he flicked it, lighting the room from a fixture on the ceiling.

The walk-up wasn't a typical Chinatown apartment; 3A was a railroad flat, three rooms back to back to back in a straight line. The first room was big, with a small bathroom in front of him to his right. An alley window and a table with chairs were to his left. Beyond that, at the far wall, was a kitchenette setup: range top, sink, small refrigerator.

The place looked like it'd had a face-lift over the last couple of decades.

He hung the bag with the carton of smokes on the front doorknob.

To his right was another narrow room, or corridor. He flicked another light switch. There was a closet on his left, a worn club chair in a nook facing a small television set with an ashtray and a pack of Marlboros on top of it.

He went into the last room, hit the switch. The bedroom was a small square with a full-size mattress bed, a small nightstand with a cheap table lamp to the right of the headboard. Along the wall to his left were a dresser with a mirror and a folding chair with folded laundry on it.

He took a settling breath and went back to the kitchenette.

He checked the refrigerator, then the cabinets. In the refrigerator freezer he found frozen dumplings and *yu don* fish balls, some red bean ice bars, and a bag of lotus seed *baos*. On the inside door there were bottles of soy sauce, oyster sauce, Sriracha. On the bottom shelf there was a brick of tofu, a package of *lop cheung* sausage, a box of salted eggs, and a can of lychees. A bottle of Absolut vodka to one side.

There was a shopping bag of plastic takeout bags on the floor next to a garbage bin. A six-pack of water bottles nearby.

In one cabinet he found bulk packs of assorted ramen and *mei fun* rice noodles. Stacks of plastic plates and cups, forks, and spoons that looked like restaurant supply. The second cabinet was emptier; it held just a small bag of rice, a box of tea bags from Ten Ren, and an assortment of sweets and candies, mango slices, and the kind of *wah moy* he'd kept in the car.

Beneath the cabinets was a sink, with a dish-drainer tray next to it. In the rack was one cup, one dish, one bowl, a pair of chopsticks, and a spoon. At the end of the counter there was a small electric rice cooker.

The range top held a wok, a teapot, and a soup pan.

So far everything indicated that Gaw's apartment was a single bachelor's setup. Jack grabbed some of the plastic takeout bags and continued.

At the wall edge of the table was a tin of Tea Time cookies, a bag of roasted Chinese peanuts. Almost covered by the bag of nuts was a can, which upon closer inspection turned out to be a can of abalone. "*Abba-lone-nay*," Jack remembered Ruben saying in Spanish. *Abalone*. He dropped the can into one of the takeout bags, leaving it on the table for the time being.

He'd hoped to find a weapon, maybe contraband, and turned his attention to the bathroom.

The mirrored medicine cabinet held Tylenol and Band-Aids and an assortment of Chinese herbal treatments and liniments like *mon gum yow* and *deet da jao*.

He checked under the sink and toilet bowl. *Clean.*

There weren't any weapons or drugs in the toilet tank.

He headed for the second room.

The middle room, with the little closet and the notch out, was the equivalent of a living room, a small area where you could sit down, watch the little TV, and have a drink or smoke a cigarette. A chill-out area before the last room, where you had sex or just went to bed.

Inside the closet was a lightbulb on a pull chain. Jack tugged on the chain and illuminated a line of clothing hanging off a rail. Shirts and jackets mostly. *Nothing in the pockets.* Above the rail was a shelf holding sheets and towels. He ran his latexed hands through the folds and along the shelf's edges.

At knee level there was an empty piece of rollaway luggage. On the floor next to it was a stack of magazines. Some Hong Kong periodicals and mail-order catalogs. The periodicals had dog-eared pages featuring recent Triad violence; he couldn't read most of the Chinese words, but the graphic news photos told the bloody stories clearly enough.

The mail-order catalogs, addressed to Gaw, had Golden Mountain Realty, Bossy's office, as the mailing address. They also had dog-eared pages. The first one was a BadZ catalog of On the Edge knives, featuring all kinds of exotic, themed, and commercialized blades from tantos to tomahawks. He thumbed through the dog-eared pages, looking for a dagger or dirk that might fit the murder weapon. He found several: the Scorpion Dagger was a four-inch blade that was compact, flat, and easily concealed. A second knife was also a dagger, *a 4.33-inch stainless-steel blade with a black rubber, water-resistant handle. Easily concealed nylon shoulder harness with sheath. $29.95.*

There was a *tactical* knife with plastic handles. It had a long blade, six inches, and the pierced handle allowed for a lanyard.

They were all cheap knives, thought Jack, probably made in China, so the steel wasn't trustworthy. He picked up the next catalog, a thicker one with a slick cover that was headlined *Sporting Knives Annual*. Featured on the cover were high-end knives, collectors' and enthusiasts' blades from mostly American and European manufacturers.

Several selections had been dog-eared.

Böker USA offered a combat knife, a Colonel Rex Applegate model. The sheath system allowed for *nine* carry positions including boot, waist, neck, hip, pocket, and jacket-pocket carry. It had a fiberglass-reinforced Delrin handle with a forward-bending crossguard and a stainless-steel, drop-point blade. *Indentations in the handle provide a nonslip, firm grip. An ideal knife that weighs only 2.3 ounces.*

Murder weapon? wondered Jack. *On order at $99.95.*

The second dog-eared choice was a cousin of the combat knife. The Buck Diamondback claimed the same quality steel on a shorter blade. *Tactile-patterned handle with quick-draw sheath.*

The last choice in the catalog was a Gerber knife. The Expedition IB offered a black-finished, 3.25-inch, high-carbon steel blade inside a glass-reinforced nylon handle. *Includes plastic, multidraw sheath. Available as double-edged or with stainless-steel finish. At $75.*

He bagged the catalogs and folded them into his jacket.

Turning to the club chair, he pulled it out and tipped it over. *Nothing underneath.* He bagged the pack of smuggled Marlboros on top of the television. The television itself was connected to a long extension cord so that it could be placed on top of the dresser. *Watch TV in bed if desired.* He ran his fingers under the TV stand. *Clear.*

He repositioned the club chair and went into the bedroom.

He flicked the wall switch, though the ceiling light was unnecessary. The bedroom, or front room, since it had windows overlooking Pell Street, was clearly lit and sparse, no clutter, the room of an orderly, *calculating* person. Jack conducted a sweep of the bed, behind the headboard, under the mattress, the box spring. *Nothing there.*

The nightstand was empty, top and bottom.

The dresser, with its fake-wood finish, had three wide drawers. The top drawer held mostly shirts and knits, a couple of sweaters, winter fashions. Blacks and grays mostly, with a few red-colored items for Chinese New Year.

He checked the edges, the bottom of the drawer.

The second drawer held mostly T-shirts, underwear, and socks in a mash-up. He ran his fingers around the edges and under the drawer.

The bottom drawer held a few pairs of shorts—watersports prints, denims—and polo shirts and poolside flip-flops. Two pairs of D&G knockoff sunglasses. Jack didn't know why, but he bagged one pair, putting it into his jacket. He thought he'd show it to Ah Por later.

He felt around the edges, the bottom of the drawer, fingering through the denim shorts, under the polo shirts next to the flip-flop sandals. He suddenly felt something hard, *a lead sap*, he wanted to believe, but it wasn't any bigger than a matchbook, though thicker. *Folding knife?* He gently spread back the shirts.

Lifting away the sandals, he saw that it was tarnished steel, a metal rectangle the size of a belt buckle. *A cigarette lighter.*

A cigarette lighter. An old one, not the modern, butane-injected kind.

He carefully took it out, stood it up on top of the dresser. It was an old Vietnam War–era Zippo lighter, the kind you could find in army-navy surplus stores on Canal Street or anywhere in the city. On one side was a grinning skull with wings. A screaming eagle decorated the other side, along with the engraved words DEATH FROM ABOVE.

Has to be Singarette's lighter, thought Jack, sucking in a breath while remembering the words of the China Village deliveryman: *Had a war eagle on it.* And cherry lady Huong, *with a say yun touh, a smiling skull, on it.*

Maybe Gaw had taken the lighter as a souvenir, a scalp, whatever. Proof, perhaps, for whoever put him up to killing Sing.

Jack remembered the Zippo lighters. They were still popular in the military during his short stint in the army. They routinely required a few squirts of lighter fluid into a fuel-sponging insert you pulled out of the casing. A refill could last a week or two. Gaw had apparently abandoned it anyway, maybe after the insert had dried out. There'd probably be fingerprints, thumb and index prints, probably Sing's, on the insert. Hopefully Gaw's and Sing's fingerprints would turn up on the outside metal casing of the Zippo. He made a mental note to advise the lab techs about the insert.

There was nothing else in the room, but he felt sure he had enough evidence to tie Gaw to Sing's murder. *Circumstantial, perhaps, but evidence nonetheless.*

He bagged the Zippo and took it, along with the bagged pack of cigarettes off the TV, as he switched off lights leaving the two rooms.

In the kitchen, he grabbed the takeout bag with the can of abalone inside, the carton of Marlboros off the doorknob. He clutched all the plastic bags together as he switched off the lights and left the apartment.

He knew he needed to get the evidence to the lab, where forensics could work it over. Since he was, so far, the lone link in the chain of custody, he decided to expedite matters by dropping the evidence off with forensics himself.

He ignored the fact that the stitches in his arm were throbbing again.

Flow

IT WAS MIDAFTERNOON by the time Jack got back to Chinatown. He was hoping that forensics would have some results on the overnight if they weren't too backed up.

He finished and submitted a report at the Fifth Precinct, describing Gaw's attack on him on the Pell Street rooftop. *Trying to kill a cop. That charge alone would keep Gaw on ice for a while.*

Singarette's case file was still open, though new evidence was surfacing. He called the mail-order-catalog companies, identifying the police investigation, and referred to the account numbers on the mailing label. He felt lucky that the supervisor was cooperative: customer 2288 (Gaw) had ordered from *Sporting Knives*—an Applegate combat knife and the Gerber Expedition. Both shipped to Golden Mountain Realty.

From the BadZ catalog he'd ordered a "Knockout" flat sap, *with five ounces of molded lead sewn into a leather shank.*

An old-school weapon, thought Jack, *also illegal to carry in the city.*

The mailing address loosely linked Bossy to the killing deal. Gaw had had weapons delivered to the office. But proving Bossy knew anything about it was another matter.

At least he had Gaw on ice at the Tombs.

He tucked the catalogs back into his jacket, left the station house, and headed for the Senior Citizens' Center, two blocks away on Bayard Street. He'd missed Ah Por the last time and wondered if she was around to apply her special touch.

Senior Secrets

HE FOUND HER right away, with a Styrofoam cup of *ha gwoo cho* tea by the side door. Free afternoon tea, enjoyed by all the seniors, sometimes included cookies that were near-expiration stock, donated by the local Chinese supermarkets.

He quickly slipped Ah Por the folded five-dollar bill, followed by the knockoff sunglasses from Gaw's dresser. It took a moment as she touched them and said, "Canal Street." *Sure, that sounds familiar,* thought Jack.

"*Som luk bot,*" she added. *Three-six-eight.*

Is she just regurgitating past answers now? wondered Jack. It was the same number clue from the Yonkers racetrack program.

He slipped her another five, passed her the Golden Mountain Realty brochure. She looked at him thoughtfully and took a gulp of the *ha gwoo cho* before running her fingers over Bossy's smiling, thumbprint-sized brochure photo.

"He will never see the rat," she said so quietly he was unsure of what he'd heard. *What?* frowned Jack. *Does she mean Bossy's going to hang Gaw out to dry?*

"What?" he muttered aloud. He took a calming breath.

"His money," Ah Por said with a sigh, "is *death* money."

She means Bossy has money to burn? he wondered.

Ah Por's attention drifted, her eyes seemingly searching for someone in the crowd.

He couldn't follow her words about Bossy, the *rat* and the *money*, but any clue that Ah Por repeated, *three-six-eight, Canal Street*, demanded attention.

He patted her on the shoulder of her *meen ngaap* jacket, smiled and nodded, and left the Seniors' Center.

He headed for Canal Street on Baxter Way, imagining a gift shop or army-surplus store.

CANAL STREET WAS a slog, with the throngs of tourists dealing with the knockoff vendors: the Fukienese *designer handbag* ladies, the Nigerian briefcase or sunglasses posse, the Pakistanis with the fake perfumes, *cubana* jewelry store, the Vietnamese moving everything under the sun.

He went past the Burger King and Mickey D's, tourist havens, past the electronics and odd-lot discount shops and surplus stores, almost to Church Street.

He was surprised.

Number 368 Canal Street was a newer Bank of America branch, a half-mile from the bank-crowded heart of Chinatown but very clear about its identity. A semicircular glass façade faced the street, like a moon gate. Inside, there were bright colors, Asian-friendly tones over a bamboo forest motif.

A flight of stairs led up to a wall of six teller stations, smiling Chinese girls behind bulletproof Plexiglas. A seating area, clean and mellow. A flight of stairs down to the safe-deposit vault. The assistant manager sat behind a desk and looked like a younger version of Bossy.

There weren't any customers around.

Jack badged him, showed him Sing's key, and asked, "Do you list Jun Wah Zhang as an account? This is a murder investigation."

The assistant manager seemed unimpressed and spoke Cantonese with a Shanghainese accent. "Don't you need a warrant or something for that?" he challenged.

"Sure, I can do that," Jack said with a smile, "but that could take all night. In the meantime I'd have to post a uniformed officer here to make sure no one goes into any of the boxes. You'll have to turn customers away. Tomorrow, too, if necessary."

The man's Adam's apple bounced a couple of times.

"Think that'll ruin your manager's dinner, his whole evening?" Jack pressed.

The assistant manager wavered, swallowed hard. He reluctantly tapped up some names from his computer keyboard, frowned, and escorted Jack to a box in a wall of small slotted boxes. He matched Sing's key to his master and opened the little cast-metal door. He slid the thin, metal safe-deposit box out and flipped open the lid.

Jack saw there were two photographs: an old snapshot of a family of three, in the faded colors of the 1970s, of young parents and an infant son, in a rural Chinese setting. The mother, in village dress, cradled the child in her arms, *precious*, smiling. The father, smiling cautiously, held a miner's helmet in one hand, resting the other on his wife's shoulder. The simple Chinese notations on the back read "Ma and Ba, 1971." The other photo was more recent, a tourist snapshot at the Statue of Liberty. Singarette, with Lady Liberty looming in the background, beaming a jubilant smile at the camera. *So happy to be in America!* The photo looked like it had been taken in the fall, November maybe, judging by the clothes worn by park rangers in the background of the picture. A posed-tourist Polaroid in a cardboard frame.

There was a China passport and student visa banded together, which he'd purchased from the real Jun Wah back in Poon Yew village.

These were the items Sing had considered most valuable, enough to keep them safe: a photo of his real family and, ironically, the passport visa he'd bought for a new future in America.

Ah Por's yellow witchery had paid off again.

Jack signed for the items, slipped them inside his jacket, and on the way out wondered if the victim's file was the right place for what was left of Sing's life. On Canal Street, the offices and commercial businesses had begun to shut down, workers anticipating the rush hour home.

Looking east, he decided to make one more visit before leaving Chinatown.

Wah Fook

"We tried to call you," the manager said as soon as he saw Jack enter the funeral parlor. "Two nights ago. He's been interred already." The manager paused. "At Saint Margaret's. There's another procession going out there in the morning. You can catch a ride out."

Jack thanked him, went to Bowery, and caught a *sai ba* to Brooklyn.

When he got back to Sunset Park, he felt emotionally exhausted, with the various injuries barking at him now. He ordered *gnow mei* noodles at one of the soup shacks on Eighth Avenue, chased it with a pain pill, and wondered what Bossy or Solomon Schwartz had up his sleeves next.

Saints

Saint Margaret's lay above Astoria Boulevard on the edge of East Elmhurst, not far from LaGuardia Airport. Both destinations were familiar to Chinatown *see gay* drivers.

It was an old cemetery, not as big as Evergreen Hills or other cemeteries in Queens, and had only a small Chinese section, mainly from Chinese families that had moved into Elmhurst during the 1970s.

The elderly groundskeeper was accommodating to Jack's badge, escorted him to the Chinese section. He saw a mash-up of Chinese surnames carved into the varied headstones protruding like crooked teeth from the hillside edge of the cemetery.

"Right there." The groundskeeper pointed at a field next to

the cemetery dump. There were no tombstones there, only small stone markers sunk into the uneven ground. *A potter's field.* Upon closer inspection, Jack saw markers that were polished, brick-sized leftovers from some wholesale rock quarry.

Gradually, he found the Chinese character for "Chang"— 張 —engraved into flat gray stone. *A respectful carving, considering it was a charity job.* Tossed to one side was a small wooden slat that the cemetery used as a temporary grave marker. The slat had JUN WAH CHANG scrawled in black Chinese script.

Jack took the piece of wood and gouged out a shallow hole next to Sing's stone marker. He'd put Sing's family photo into a Ziploc bag and now placed it in his final resting place. Jack covered it over carefully and tamped down the ground with his hands.

He lit the three sticks of incense he'd gotten from the funeral driver and bowed three times. *Rest in peace*, he offered silently.

The sky seemed to brighten on the drive back to Chinatown.

He got the driver to let him off on Canal Street, across from the market vendors on Mulberry. He could see the colorful displays of fruit, the cherry stand, on the other side of the busy boulevard.

At the cherry stand, Huong was surprised to see him and knew it wasn't a social visit.

"You've found justice for Sing?" she asked. Jack silently nodded *yes* as she took a breath, covered her mouth with her hand.

"He was a good man," she said, shaking her head.

"He's buried in Queens, under the name Chang," Jack

said. "Not much of a cemetery for Chinese. But anyway, I thought he'd want you to have this." He handed her Sing's Statue of Liberty photo.

There was sadness behind the happiness in her eyes as she stared at the photo. She took a calming breath, said, "This is the way I like to remember Sing. Smiling at the world." She gave Jack a glance and a small smile.

"Thank you, Detective," she said. "I can put this in my family's temple. We can say prayers for him on all the holidays, and on his birthday."

Which is Saint Patrick's Day, Jack remembered, *a few weeks away.*

"And I still owe you a lunch," he said.

"I haven't forgotten."

"Just let me know what place you like," Jack added.

Huong smiled sadly and pocketed the photo as a group of tourists approached to buy cherries.

"I'll let you know," she answered as he backed away and turned with a wave goodbye.

Somehow he didn't feel that date was going to happen, that they'd already come to the end of the chapter. He was almost to Bayard Street when his cell phone jangled. It was Sarge from the Fifth, a garbled connection from which Jack understood only the word "forensics."

He was just two blocks west of the station house.

Fax Facts

THE WORDS TRANSFIXED Jack as he read the fax copy of the forensics report.

They'd found nothing matching on the can of abalone. There were only Gaw's prints on the pack of Marlboros taken from his apartment.

Jack frowned as he kept reading.

On the carton of Marlboros taken from Gaw's Town Car, there *was* a match on both Gaw's and Sing's fingerprints.

They'd both handled the carton at some point.

On the Zippo lighter, they'd found only Sing's fingerprints on the insert, but *both* Gaw's and Sing's prints on the metal case.

Killer and victim linked again.

Jack had gotten two hits out of four. If this were baseball, he mused, he'd be considered a star. He felt the urge to squeeze Gaw about how he'd happened to be in possession of Singarette's lighter, hidden in the apartment.

Not that he would be expecting an answer.

Jacked

AT THE TOMBS, Jack was greeted by somber black faces.

"Immigration came by," the one named Ingram said with a frown.

"INS agents, on the overnight," said Crawford, the tall one.

"They chained him and *jacked* him, man," added Johnson, the youngest.

Immigration and Naturalization Service. Their agents were mostly law enforcement from other federal branches, sometimes military, but usually veteran officers. A big part of INS work was transporting criminal immigrants.

He knew two cold-case homicides trumped an attempted

murder of a New York City cop and a *possible* homicide, but someone must've wanted Gaw really bad for INS to jack him out of the Tombs in the dead of night, within seventy-two hours of detention. *Over a murder case, no less.*

He knew it would jam his investigation to a halt.

"Did they say where he was going?" Jack asked.

"To Hong Kong," Ingram answered. "Said he was going to meet *Chinese* justice."

Jack nodded acknowledgment, knowing Chinese justice could mean a "Beijing haircut," a nine-millimeter, hollow-point bullet to the head, ripping out the bad brains. *Life is cheap in China.* Then they'd bill the criminal's family for the bullet.

Or it could mean years in a dark, airless cell.

Or it could mean disappearing inside the Chinese prison system, where maybe, with the Triad's help paying off the warden and guards, Gaw would be set free. Free to resume his Triad life.

Or they just might decide it's cheaper to shank him to death in prison, if rival Triads didn't get him first.

Jack wondered if Bossy had his fingerprints on any of it. Wondered if the Hip Chings were connected somehow. *Screw it*, he decided, marching to Mott and Pell.

Bossy's office.

He didn't know if Bossy'd be there, but Jack pressed the button anyway. The receptionist buzzed him in and tried to stall him, but he barged into Bossy's office and caught him by surprise.

Bossy coolly waved the indignant receptionist away, her cue to visit the ladies' room. Jack gave her until the sound of the closing door before he began.

"Weapons were shipped to your office," he said. "Probably your pretty secretary signed for them."

Bossy maintained his frozen smile, clenched his fists, raised an eyebrow.

"Your driver Gaw's good for the killing," Jack continued. "And maybe I can't prove it now, but I know you had a hand in it somehow. Maybe you got over on me, but it all comes back around, *you know*? And with your family's history, I'm sure you know what that means."

Bossy smirked, declined to dignify anything Jack had said with a response. He folded his arms, leaned back, and waited for Jack to leave.

The phone rang outside, and the receptionist quickly reappeared, throwing fearful looks in Jack's direction. She answered the call but didn't relax until he finally left Bossy's office, her eyes following him until he turned and went down the stairs. He didn't care about the surveillance camera on the wall or worry about Internal Affairs breathing down his neck.

Sing's case was a matter of record now, and there's wasn't anything Bossy could do to alter that.

Golden Star

THE PARTY AT Grampa's was spur of the moment, with Jack having spread the word through Huong and giving the Tombs cops a heads-up. It was a raucous, alcohol-fueled scene, occupying the booths along the side wall, with the Commodores and Isley Brothers jamming loud on the jukebox.

Grampa's kitchen served the party plates of clams casino, fried chicken wings, and Chef Kim's signature onion-smothered steaks and chops.

Jack threw the party at Grampa's knowing a few extra blacks and Latinos weren't going to raise any eyebrows here. He was happy to see his African American Tombs brother cops—Ingram, Crawford, and Johnson—enjoying cocktails in the second booth and digging the music. It occurred to Jack how much Ingram, Crawford, and Johnson sounded like a law firm.

He started his second boilermaker. *Payback is a bitch, like they say.* The party was small thanks for those who'd helped on Sing's case.

He'd invited Ruben, Miguel, and Luis—the *tres amigos*—sitting in the third booth. *Cervezas* all around, and smoking up a storm cloud. The three Mexican truckmen seemed to fit well with the *Loisaida Boricua* regulars at Grampa's.

He leaned back and imagined the headline scoop he owed Vincent Chin and the *United National*: KILLER OF CHINESE DELIVERYMAN EXTRADITED TO HONG KONG FOR PAST CRIMES. *They'd have to do* dim sum *sometime.* Taking a gulp of the icy beer, he still marveled at Ah Por's *bank* clue. *More yellow Taoist witchcraft.* He fired up a cigarette and considered how his stitches weren't pulling so much anymore. The boilermakers were beginning to scatter his thoughts, and the jukebox thundered on.

The only one who seemed out of sorts was Billy Bow, who sat across from Jack in the corner booth. Billy scarfed down a baked clam and chased it with some Dewar's.

"So it boils down to stinky tofu," he said, wrinkling his nose. "One Chinaman with a paper name snuffs another

Chinaman with a paper name, both here *illegally* mind you, and no one except you really gives a shit how they jacked the killer back to China? *Man*, that's fucked up."

Billy had a way of putting things, especially when he'd had a few drinks. His words held some truth, however. Gaw and Sing were two invisible men who no one paid much attention to. One eked out a living on the edges of the restaurant industry. *His invisibility got him killed.* The other was a Triad criminal hiding in plain sight for twenty years. *He cultivated his invisibility, and it allowed him to kill.*

If Gaw hadn't killed Sing, their lives would have gone on, almost predictably, and no one would have even known they existed.

Jing deng, Jack mused, *destiny.* Always in control.

Billy took another slug of the Dewar's, turned his cynicism toward the rest of the party.

"Too many niggas and spics here tonight," he muttered.

"Billy, *stop*," Jack said. "They all helped me during the case. Just like you did."

"Yeah, but . . . I know, but . . ." He shook his head.

"So *relax*, all right?" Jack pleaded. "Have another drink." Then he leaned in, spoke just loud enough to be heard, "And don't be such a fucking hater, okay?"

Before Billy could protest, Jack gave him a brotherly pat across the shoulders.

"And remember," Jack continued. "I owe you a date at Chao's."

Billy brightened immediately, the thought of pussy erasing the racist spike in his brain. "That's *right*!" he remembered alcoholically.

"*All* right," Jack reinforced the change in mood, buying

Billy another round. *Better drunk than sorry*. He could always get someone at Grampa's to take Billy home if necessary.

By the third boilermaker, Jack began to put together what Ah Por's witchy words actually meant. The *rat* could be a reference to the Year of the Rat, the coming year in the Chinese horoscope. *Ten months away*. Ah Por meant *Bossy won't see the next year?* If so, according to her words, it'd be true that Bossy's fortune was nothing more than *death money*. *He'd never be able to spend it fast enough*. The largesse would be left to whom? His Taiwanese wife? His gangster-wannabe son?

Maybe justice traveled in a slower circle, pondered Jack.

He watched Billy take his scotch to the pool table in the back, where a vampy white girl was waiting to hustle a willing fish like him.

Ruben was the first to leave, followed by Johnson. As the party wound down, Jack stopped keeping track of who left. By 1 A.M. the pace had slowed to a drunken slog. He didn't see Billy anywhere and signed his running tab before leaving Grampa's.

He was home by 2 A.M., noting the time display on the clock radio before collapsing onto his bed.

Backup

JACK AWOKE TO a brilliant morning, shaking off the lingering haze from the night's boilermakers. He knew the sky was brilliant by the bright light knifing in at the edges of his shaded windows. He turned on the TV, surfed the channels until he came to local news, an item featuring the Lantern

Festival in Chinatown. *Chinese schoolchildren parading with lanterns around Chinatown.*

He muted the sound, reached for his cell phone, which was vibrating on the nightstand.

There were two messages that he'd missed during the noisy scene at Grampa's. The first one was from a Ninth Precinct number, an NYPD shrink named May McMann, about rescheduling an appointment.

The second message was from a number he didn't know, but he recognized Alexandra's voice right away.

"Heyyy, let's meet at Tsunami, at four P.M." *Curt, to the point.* He hadn't seen her in more than a week.

When he tried to call the number back, all he got was disconnect.

He powered the audio back, watched as candlelit Chinese lanterns floated down Mott Street followed by a marching band from the Chinese school. Many businesses hung lanterns above their doors, inviting luck for the new year.

Then he thought about Sing. *Singarette*, who would have turned twenty-four this year. *Yee say*, the numbers whispered, twenty-four sounding like *easy to die* in Cantonese.

The images of Sing, from the river to the grave, tumbled in his brain. He didn't think anyone would visit Sing at Saint Margaret's, but he knew that cherry lady Huong would offer prayers and memorials at the Buddhist temple.

He won't be forgotten.

On the TV screen, the Chinatown religious and civic groups marched along, joined by a contingent of Chinese auxiliary police officers.

He got up and looked at his stitches in the mirror, the

jagged lines scabbing over now. He'd lose the stitches in a few days, he knew.

Not in a celebratory mood, he turned off the TV and lay back down on the bed. He couldn't reconcile the mixed feelings in his head. Though he was happy that he'd caught Sing's killer, the arrest felt hollow. Mak Mon Gaw might yet get justice, but for other crimes. *And Bossy'd gotten away scot-free, at least for now.* According to Ah Por, Bossy wasn't going to make it to the next lunar New Year. *We'll see,* thought Jack.

He closed his eyes and tried to quiet the chatter inside his head. He imagined the patchy ground of the potter's field at Saint Margaret's and the mourning sounds of an *erhu* far off in the distance.

Come Back

TSUNAMI WAS A sushi joint, located where the Lower East Side melted into the East Village, walking distance from Alex's AJA storefront. They had a sushi bar where the fish snacks circulated around on a conveyor belt. You could order cold soba or hot udon or kushiyaki on the side.

He and Alex had celebrated there a couple of times before.

He pictured Alex's pretty face. It'd been a week since he'd seen her, almost two weeks since they last made love. Coming straight out of Brooklyn by *see gay*, he hadn't had the chance to stop in Chinatown to get her something sweet from Mott Street.

He was considering where to sit, bar or booth, when she walked in.

Alex gave him a peck on the cheek and ushered him into one of the empty booths, sliding in behind him. *She looks great*, he thought, *something edgy around her eyes*.

She ordered two large bottles of filtered sake as they settled in, a body distance between them that allowed them to look directly into each other's eyes. Clearly happy to see each other.

They toasted a shot of the little sake cups, each catching a breath. Then the words poured out of her mouth, through the lips he remembered kissing tenderly. What she said stunned him, hit him harder than a lead sap, harder than a hundred-pound sack of rice.

"We have to back it up," she said, locking his eyes. "Not see each other. For a while at least."

He was speechless, wanted to protest, but knew to let her tell it.

"The son of a bitch," she said with a frown. He knew she meant her soon-to-be ex-husband. "He somehow got a copy of a security tape from Confucius Towers."

"No," Jack said quietly, now understanding the edge he'd seen in her eyes when she walked in. She was the bearer of bad news.

"*Yes*. It shows you and me in the elevator, going up."

"No," he repeated, clenching his fists and taking a steadying breath through his nose.

"Yes. And it shows *you*," she continued, "going back down *alone*."

Before dawn, remembered Jack, the last time they'd made love. He downed his cup of sake, poured another. Her words made him feel awful, killed his appetite for sushi.

"He's threatening to use the tape against me in the

custody fight. Paint me as an unfaithful wife and unfit mother." He felt helpless and guilty, didn't know whether to apologize or add to her anger.

Jack's fist tightened around the sake bottle as he poured her another cup. She drained it before continuing.

"I'm threatening a lawsuit against Confucius Towers and Tower Security," she added. "But I don't know if that'll work."

"Everyone suffers," Jack said with a frown. "Especially the kid." The divorce demands had driven a wedge between them. *Should they have waited before giving in to their needs? She*, a lawyer, should have known better. *He* certainly knew better. Billy had warned him countless times.

"It's my fault, isn't it?" he offered.

"It's nobody's fault, Jack. He's just an evil bastard."

He reached across and took her fingers in his, caressed them as he tried to comfort her. He wanted to hold her, tell her it was going to be all right, but knew she'd passed there already. *She was trying to get ready for a fight she didn't feel was going to go her way.* They eyed each other with apprehension and sorrow.

"What can I do to help?" he asked.

She pulled her fingers away, poured herself a refill.

"The best thing you can do is to stay away from him in every way," she said. "The last thing I need is you stalking him, anything *crazy* like that." Her words cut through him, made him feel helpless to help her—this woman with whom he'd started to feel there could be a future—made him wish Lucky wasn't in a coma and could arrange the dirty work.

Jack shook his head as she contemplated the little sake cup, before throwing it back.

"And we can't be seen together," she said quietly. *That's*

why she chose Tsunami, Jack realized, *it was out of the way, outside Chinatown. They'd have to lay low.*

He didn't want to lose her. He cared more about her than anything else in his life, certainly more than anything in his cop life.

She leaned in and kissed him.

"It's over, Jack," she said, sliding out of the booth, her hand holding him back from following her. "For now." She hesitated a moment, adding, "I've changed my cell phone number. But you know where to find me." She meant at AJA, Jack knew.

She brushed a final stroke on his cheek and left the sushi joint.

He thought he saw tears welling in her eyes. He stayed back like she'd asked, watching her through the restaurant window with the big crashing wave overlay. She'd make her own way back to Chinatown and Confucius Towers, he knew, as she climbed into a cab. The passenger window rolled down, and the kiss she blew him almost broke his heart.

He had to trust what she was doing, that it was the right thing. For both of them.

He ordered another sake, drained the previous one. The rice wine smoothed the way for the pain in his stitches and bruises to mix now with the ache in his heart.

He hated the feeling of helplessness, unable to affect the consequences of what amounted to falling in love. Alex. *Alexandra. Falling in love?*

He worked the sake down, and with the afternoon light fading outside, he fired up a cigarette and deeply hoped, against his glowing cynicism, that there'd be more chapters to their story.

Acknowledgments

Kowtowing thanks to Bronwen Hruska at Soho Press, for letting me rejoin the pack, and to my editor Mark Doten, whose insight has made for a better book. A big shout-out to the entire Soho crew for their multitalented ways.

Much love to my NYC Chinatown *hingdaai*, my posse brothers, for always taking my back. To Doris Chong, as always, for the inspiration. To my agents Dana Adkins and Debbie Phillips, who continue to champion my stories. To Hong Hom, for helping me probe the cultural depths. To Jackie McCaffrey, for her vision and loyalty. To Andrew Chang and Patrick Lee, for the tech support. To Mimi, Bobo, and Fanny, for keeping my head straight. To Diana Koo for her generous support. To Charles V. Johnston III and David Beaudry, for the *chi*.

And last but most of all, gratitude to Lucas Koo and Shemy Ayon, for hanging tough and always keeping the faith.